THE COLD

SIDE

OF THE GRILL

Based on a True Story

Nick Rabar

To my loving Wife Tracy, my Children & Family

TABLE OF CONTENTS

CHAPTER 1

MY NAME IS STEVE

"Come on guys, what the fuck do I have to do to get those stuffed soles, move it! Also picking up two shrimp cocktail, two calamari, four house salads and make it snappy goddammit!" Phil shouted until he was beet red in the face. These fits were generally coupled with a sauté pan being flung across the room, and if you were lucky, it wasn't being thrown at you. "These entree times are too long, move your asses!"

The sounds of clanking stainless steel pots and the distinctive ping of porcelain plates filled the air. The door to the dining room squeaked every time it opened as servers constantly raced in and out of the kitchen. As it opened, you could feel the energy of a full and feverish restaurant pouring into the kitchen, even if just for a second before the door swung closed. Phil pounded his bellhop's bell and screamed servers' names as their food was ready. "Nicki you're up, Ena coming up on table 13, guys pick up the pace and do it now!" It was a Saturday night at Padrino's Café and it was intense with pressure and hustle. I had the unique distinction of being the dishwasher of this bustling eatery. My fingertips looked like prunes, my white button-down dishwasher's coat was wet from my chest down, I was stuck in the corner of a scorching hot kitchen covered in sweat, and I just kept my head down and tried to do my job. "Sauté pans now Jack, right now!"

"Yes sir," I screamed as I jumped from the dish machine to the three bay sink. I scrubbed those pans faster than anyone, never stopping to think, just reacting to the pressure-packed atmosphere. This is what nights were like there, full of action, demanding, and just plain vigorous. It was the type of place where you hit the ground running and didn't stop until the storm was over. Working as a dishwasher for my first job, I learned quickly that washing dishes was a solitary place; you were isolated from the rest of the kitchen, and people flew in and out and barely took time to learn your name, especially when you looked like I did.

I was a tall skinny kid, pale-skinned with freckles, glasses and straight hair named Jackson Cahill. I begged for my first job at the little restaurant in my hometown of Pleasant Valley, New York. It was a very *in* place, run by popular local kids ranging from athletes to big men on campus. Padrino's was by definition a very basic restaurant, nothing too exciting in the culinary world but a fun place to work and a good place to learn the ropes. A dedicated man named Phil owned the restaurant and took his business very seriously. Most of the staff did their jobs, and those who didn't, Phil had no qualms about letting them know it—often in a fit of rage that led to their inevitable firing. He chewed gum at an alarming rate, wore white clothes head to toe, and was very protective of Padrino's reputation. He worked hard to make sure it stayed consistent, which is the single hardest thing to maintain in this business.

Phil's staff, the good ones at least, were behind him and did as they were told. Some were pro-active, going above and beyond their day-to-day duties, while others did what they needed to so Phil wouldn't explode on them. I always kept to myself, worked hard, and did what I was told—which was easy, considering that for my first few weeks no one knew I was even there.

Eventually though, someone decided to make contact with me: a 75-year-old, 4'11" tall waitress named Ena, who probably weighed 85 pounds. One night Ena turned to me and said, "Your name is Steve, right?"

Thinking that I would like her to know my real name, I replied, "Yes, my name is Steve." I guess I just didn't want her to feel stupid by correcting her, so I went along with it.

She said, "Steve, I know this is your first day, but can you separate the forks from the spoons, 'cause in the dining room we don't have time to fiddle."

Considering I had been there for weeks, and not really knowing why she thought it was my first day, I respectfully played along and said, "No forks will be near no spoons." Without a response she turned and left. I couldn't believe what I had said. I know it wasn't a big deal, but what the hell? Was I from the fucking Mississippi backwoods? "No forks will be near no spoons?" Was I a goddamn idiot? The first time I really speak to someone and it sounds like I *should* be washing pots for the rest of my life! Live and learn I guess.

It went on like that for a while, but people slowly started to take notice and finally began to call me by name. I did my best to be helpful, always offering to assist the crew and jump in when they needed me. Most people were pretty receptive to my gestures but there were always some who had a *do it myself* attitude. I realized early on this was an industry loaded with big egos; you have to learn quickly how to deal with them and try not to piss too many people off along the way.

Eventually, after months of hard work Phil gave me a chance to work on the hot line which was where I really wanted to be. He liked me because I did my job and did it well. Once he gave me that opportunity I picked things up quickly. Cooking immediately felt natural, the motions, the timing, the challenges and responses to pressure, it was instantly appealing and I became addicted. I also warmed to the social aspect of the business; where I had been timid around girls before, I slowly developed my own swagger and became a confident flirt with the waitresses who worked there. It was common; internal fraternization was not frowned upon in restaurants, and in fact it was encouraged. I made passes and flirted with girls who were generally way out of my league but were somehow attracted to my abilities in the kitchen. Cooks have power and an identity, and being a chef was the identity I wanted. I began to crave it and quickly knew it was for me.

In a matter of time the restaurant business began to consume me; it trumped other priorities like friends, family and school. Padrino's, though a not groundbreaking restaurant, had become my life. I learned everything I could to get ahead, reading cookbooks, watching cooking programs on TV, practicing at home—often to my mother's kitchens despair. It was all encompassing and I didn't care about much else.

I worked at Padrino's for all my high school years. About halfway through my senior year Phil sold the restaurant to Chris, his head chef. Chris was a good guy; we partied together a lot, partying was a big part of the allure of the kitchen. We all worked hard together, put out perfect food that was clean and timely all night, and afterwards we ended up somewhere to drink and unwind. All of the cooks there were years older then me, they were all smoking pot, cigarettes and drinking all night long. It wasn't long before I started to as well, it was all part of the culture and I liked it. Along the way I went from a clean-cut, soft-spoken, church-going boy to a much more confident and centered individual. I had zero interest in school, but maximum interest in work. School suffered but I didn't care; it had lost all its cachet and the results showed. My parents Linda and Silvio, who were always supportive and caring, thought I was becoming a bit of a drifter. Maybe I was in some ways, but in others I was finding myself. It's funny how you may not even realize how deeply imbedded into a lifestyle you have become until you take a minute to come up for air. I loved it; each day spent in the kitchen pulled me closer to where I wanted to be and closer to the types of people I wanted to be with. Towards the end of my senior year I had grown into a talented cook, one with little direction prior to finding the restaurant world, but with a new focus. The only question I had was what to do with it. Chris had some ideas.

"It's The Culinary Institute of America," he said, unloading large bags of flour from a pallet. Deliveries would come and go all day; we were always receiving product and putting it away.

"It's close to here? How did I not know about this school?" I said, kneading some dough into pizza portions.

"Yeah man, you never heard of the Culinary?"

"No, I guess I've heard of it. I just never listened about it."

"It's a pretty goddamn good school. I think it may even be the best in the country. Remember Greg D. who used to be here a while back? He went there, and now he's working at a resort in Aspen. He's making pretty good money too, I bet."

"Colorado huh, how'd he get that job?" I was intrigued.

"The school man, there's people there from all over the world. It's a pretty big school Jack, you really should look into it."

Listening to Chris talk, I became more and more interested and decided to talk to my parents about it. They were upset that I wasn't applying to any schools up until that point; maybe this would cheer them up.

"A chef, huh?" My father had a concerned look on his face. "Chefs work a lot of hours and only a few make it really big. There are other careers out there; you don't have to take the first one you think of."

"Silvio, he has found something he likes, don't discourage the boy." We were sitting down to dinner. "Jack, if you want to be a chef, why don't we go look at the Culinary Institute in Hyde Park? It's supposedly the best school for chefs, maybe you'd like it," my mother said.

"That's kind of what I was thinking," I said, serving myself.

"Do you know how much that school costs?" my father said. You could see him doing the math in his head. He was always worried about money.

"How about we take you out to dinner there next week," my mother said with excitement. "You can see the campus and maybe we can even take a tour. I would be so proud if my baby became a big famous chef one day! Let's go on Friday."

"All right Ma, I'd like that."

"My baby, the chef," she said proudly. "I like the sound of that."

I had no idea what to expect when we visited the CIA in August. I had never put much thought into college. I didn't even know what to look for in a school. I had spent my whole senior year in the kitchen, not really thinking ahead.

"Welcome to the Culinary Institute of America, located in beautiful upstate New York!" The tour guide was really short but with a strong build, and she wore a full chef's uniform: black pants, black shoes, a crisp white chef jacket with a double row of buttons and a tall, cylindrical hat. She wore a kerchief tied around her neck and her hair tied back in a tight ponytail.

She spoke with a Southern accent, and she was really boring to listen to for two hours. I kind of tuned her out and just looked around instead. The campus was beautiful and had a perfect view of the Hudson River that ran right past it. It was impressively landscaped with gorgeous 19th century style buildings as halls. Besides the dorms, there were several buildings; mostly all brick and they were clean and well kept. The main student building was Roth Hall; it was five stories tall with schoolhouse windows all along the facade and large white pillars that flanked the main entrance. Everyone inside was in uniform. There were many tours being given that day and I watched as students worked in classrooms with windows on all sides. From the outside it was like watching fish swimming in fishbowls. You could observe everything going on in each room. Everyone maintained a high level of professionalism both in the classroom and in the halls.

The main dining room was something out of a storybook. It had huge cathedral ceilings with large stained-glass windows, long drapes and giant chandeliers. The table settings had Old World charger plates preset with white table linen, real silver utensils and crystal glassware. The floor was carpeted corner to corner with plush orange patterned carpet that didn't have one stain on it despite the room feeding so many people daily. There was a buffet spread that must have been 200 feet long and was impeccably presented. I had a hard time distinguishing what was food and what wasn't; everything was so petite and elegantly plated. The food was so regal and it was all prepared and served by students. My mother was thrilled to be there, she really got into it. She helped herself to the great food and had her arm around me the whole time.

"Do you know how much this school costs?" my father said, looking up at the ceilings.

"I bet it's not cheap," I said. He shot me a look.

"You asked, Pop," I said, shrugging my shoulders. He turned and kept looking around.

After we ate from the outstanding buffet, we went on to finish the tour. Walking out of Roth Hall, I felt ready. I knew this was I wanted to do. This place seemed big, people seemed sure of themselves. Everyone walked like they were getting ahead with each step. It had the right attitude.

"What do you think sweetheart, you want to get some paperwork, we can fill it out in the library before dinner?" My mother was practically packing my suitcases already.

"I'm in."

My father shook his head sadly. "This place isn't going to be cheap."

We stayed for dinner at the Caterina de' Medici, the school's Italian concept and one of the school's four restaurants. It was the smallest by far, but was still the finest restaurant I had dined in to that moment. We were greeted by a well-dressed but very short maître d instructor and seated quickly. The artwork was minimal, very understated, but it all appeared to be authentic. The room was very dark and the furnishings were all black, and dressed with white tablecloths and napkins. The students wore black and white uniforms with the schools signature green butler aprons and bow ties. They all moved with purpose and though there were many of them in such a small space, they almost disappeared into the ambiance.

The first thing that took me by surprise was the menu. I couldn't find veal parmesan or fried zucchini, and I didn't see any alfredo sauces. It was totally different than Padrino's. The menu was so elaborate, it was even written in Italian.

I had no idea that food could be so intricate. It made Padrino's look smaller in my eyes. Why weren't we doing things like squid ink pasta, octopus carpaccio and risotto? Honestly I didn't even know what they were, but they seemed so worldly and the menu seemed so dynamic, it made me question for the first time the caliber of restaurant I worked in, and started to see a bigger picture beyond pizza and calzones.

The pleasant, outgoing waiter introduced himself as a student from Vietnam. When my mother told him I was considering applying, he spoke about the school very highly. He explained that it was a tough school, and classes were long, and students have very little time for anything but school. "You either sink or swim here," he said with a slight accent.

"Are the classes really 13 hours long?" I asked.

"They really are." He was opening a bottle of wine for my parents. "You have to really want to do this in order to succeed here. It's a serious atmosphere and they don't tolerate any slacking off. If you miss even one day of a class, you automatically fail it."

"That's pretty strict," I replied.

"Well, for guys like you and me it's no big deal." He said teasing with me.

"I would have to agree," I replied confidently.

"Right on sir. Enjoy your meals, folks."

Dinner was amazing from start to finish, the flavors, the presentations, the service was like nothing I had ever experienced. I wanted to learn how to do all of it. I was convinced and began my application the next day. It wasn't easy; I needed two industry letters of recommendation, which Phil and Chris gladly provided, a 1,000-word essay describing why I felt I should be accepted into the CIA, verification of industry experience, and of course the general information application. A couple of weeks later I received my acceptance letter indicating that I would start in January, five months away. I was so disappointed. I really wanted to go right then.

All of a sudden, life around me seemed so insignificant. I still had great friends, a job I loved and a close family, but it all seemed very small, and the CIA seemed big. I couldn't imagine what my life would be like for the next few months, making fried chicken and marinara sauce all day? At this point, I just felt I needed and wanted more, and sometimes in life, luck has a funny way of intervening.

A couple of days later, I got a call from the CIA. They said they'd put my name on a waiting list for the summer and there was an opening. The term started in two days.

That was quick; two days would be all the time I had to switch from where I was to where I wanted to be. I thought about it and realized that it was now or never and I was ready. I called the school right back and accepted. I'd made up my mind. I was going to college.

The day before classes began I had much to accomplish. I had to get my uniforms, pick up my books and knife kit, go to the bursar's office to officially enroll, and take care of all of the little things involved with starting at a new school. I had a list a mile long. I also had to learn my way around the campus so I'd know where to go for classes the next day.

It was a beautiful summer day and I got to campus around noon. I had to check in at the front desk and register. Normally you have to register months ahead of time, but I was an exception because I'd only got called the day before. I filled out everything I needed to and hustled up to the bursar's office. The line was up and down the hallway with students who all seemed pretty friendly. People were laughing and having conversations. It looked like a nice group of people who were all getting to know each other.

"Jesus you scared me!" The guy turned around, startled to see me standing there. "I mean, you didn't scare me, I just didn't think anyone was behind me. Sorry."

"That's OK, I have that effect on most people," I said cleverly.

He laughed. He stuck out his hand to shake mine and said, "I doubt it man, you seem cool. What's your name bro?"

"I'm Jack, Jack Cahill." I shook his hand.

"Well Jack, Jack Cahill, I'm Tom. It's nice to meet you man."

"Yeah, I bet it is," I said kidding with him. "It's nice to meet you too."

"I know it is," he joked back. He had a smooth and sly way of speaking. He was about 5'10, 180 pounds, in good shape. "So Jack, where you from?"

"Right here. I live about 20 minutes from campus."

"That's convenient; you probably know the area pretty well."

"Yeah, I guess so."

"Hey Karen, get over here." He was waving his hand to signal her over. "Come on babe, I got to show you something."

I watched a woman break through the line of people. Now, I don't remember everything that has happened in my life. I don't remember my first steps, I don't remember my first hit in a baseball game, or the day I took the training wheels off my bike. But I remember the first time I laid eyes on Karen Macrillo. The world seemed to turn into slow motion, and everyone in the background just seemed to disappear. She was the most amazing thing I'd ever seen in my life. She walked with an incredible smile on her face, tossing her hair over her shoulder. It was like a scene right out of a movie. She had short, lightly curled brown hair, sky blue eyes, and perfect skin. She was so sophisticated, dressed in a shin-length skirt and an astonishing close-fitting russet top. She was an absolute vision.

"Hi," she said, seemingly delighted to meet me. I was speechless.

"Karen, this is Jack. Jack is from right around town. I'm sure he can tell you how to get to the mall from here."

"Yeah, I bet he could. I think I'll save him the trouble though, 'cause I think it's only two miles down Route 9, right Jack?" She smiled in my direction, turning me into a puddle.

"Uh..."

"How'd you find out babe?" Tom interrupted before I could respond in actual words.

"Molly was there this morning, she already gave me directions. Thanks anyway honey," she said, patting Tom's belly. She smiled and turned away. "It was nice meeting you Jack." She gave me a wave and left. She seemed very free-spirited.

"Nice to meet you too," I managed. My voice slowly faded as I watched her leave. Tom was also looking at her, so I don't think he noticed me drooling.

"That's your girlfriend, huh Tom?" I asked in disbelief.

"Yeah, man, that's my girl," he said, taking a deep breath as if he couldn't believe it himself.

"Where you guys from?" I asked.

"Well, I'm from North Carolina and she's from Delaware. We both got here two weeks ago. She was moving in so I asked her if she needed help. She accepted and the two of us got to talking. Turns out we don't have a lot in common except looks, so we don't do a lot of talking, if you know what I mean." He smirked.

"You mean you didn't know each other before here?"

"No, why do you ask?" he said, folding his arms.

"Well, you two seem pretty close already, that's all. You seem like you've been together for a while," I was stuttering a bit.

"Well we haven't, but you're right, we are pretty close."

"Cool man, she seems nice."

"Well, nice to meet you Jack Cahill. I'm sure I'll see you around."

I walked down the stairs of Roth Hall. As I walked out the front door, I paused to look around and as I did, Karen popped into my head. I was officially a student at this point and so was she. I couldn't get too preoccupied with her, though; after all, she seemed pretty happy with Tom and he appeared to be a decent guy. I got it out of my head, got into my car and drove home. Tomorrow was going to be a big day.

CHAPTER 2

A BLOCK

August 17th, 1996, fewer than six weeks after high school graduation, I was officially going to college. I chose to lay low the night before because I didn't want to go out and party. I wanted to have a clear head for my first day of classes. Everyone seemed so much older and more mature there. I didn't want to get a bad rap on my first day.

The school wasn't like most colleges. We didn't really have semesters and classes that ran for months at a time, we had blocks. The average block was three weeks long, A Block was the first and it went on sequentially from there. Some consisted of two classes, each eight days in length. Others were just three-week-long classes, no matter what the days were promised to be long and the curriculum intense.

The A Block uniform was black pants, socks, shoes, and belt, a white-collar shirt, and a solid-colored tie. We couldn't have much facial hair; we were allowed sideburns if they were less than half an inch in length, and a mustache cut above the lip. Only two pieces of jewelry were allowed—a wedding band and a watch. Our shoes had to be polished every day, and we had to be well tucked in at all times. Walking the halls in our A Block uniforms we stood out, because everyone else after A Block was dressed in chef whites. It was a sort of "welcome to the club but not so fast," like a 3-week fraternity hazing, but you were in it with your whole class so at least you go through it together. Nobody took it too hard, but it was a good chance for people in B Block and beyond to give us funny looks as we walked by.

That morning I woke up, made some coffee, put on my A Block uniform, and took my first ride to school. Class began at 7:00, which was normally pretty early for me, but that day I wasn't tired. I was too excited to be tired. I walked up the stairs of Roth Hall, up two more flights of stairs, and headed to Room 203A, Culinary Math 101. A Block consisted of two classes, culinary math and introduction to gastronomy, which is the study of food. My schedule was math from 7:00 to 11:00, and gastronomy from noon to 3:00.

As I approached the classroom, I saw a bunch of people standing outside in the hall. Since I didn't know anyone, I just headed into class. A few people said hello to me, which was nice. The room was filled with excited students dressed in their black and whites. Some people were talking, others sitting quietly. I looked around and saw Tom with his back to the door talking to Karen and another girl. The desks were like small tables for two, and the chair next to Tom was free.

"Anybody sitting here, man?" I asked, trying not to interrupt.

"No bro, take a seat," he responded pleasantly. "You remember Karen, right?"

"Yeah, it's nice to see you again," I said, trying not to gawk at her. She looked so good, even in a shirt and tie with her beautiful hair tied back.

"Same here Jack, how are you?"

"Good thanks." I sat down next to Tom.

"Jack, this is my friend Molly."

"Hi Molly, it's nice to meet you."

"Nice to meet you too, Jack." She smiled as I shook her hand.

The four of us all kind of smiled at each other. There were a couple of seconds of awkward silence before anyone said anything. Molly kept glancing in my direction. She was a cute girl from Michigan with short, dirty-blonde hair and chubby cheeks. I thought she was attractive, but I hardly even noticed with Karen sitting next to her.

While I was looking around the room at my new class-mates, Mr. Goldstein, the professor, walked in. He was short, bald, and wore a typical math teacher's suit. The room got quiet as he approached his desk. He put his brief-case down, put on his glasses and said, "Good morning A Blockers. My name is Mr. Goldstein. Welcome to Culinary Math 101. Some of you will enjoy this class, and others of you will not. You will be prompt every day, you will have your assignments on my desk before I walk through that door completed in their entirety, and you will be tested on them as well. Any questions feel free to ask, but don't waste your, or even worse, my time with the obvious. Do we understand each other my little wannabe chefs of America?"

"Yes sir, Mr. Goldstein," the class said in unison.

"Good. Then let's get started. And by the way, I don't like apples, so save 'em for the bakeshop. This is math. You got me?"

Mr. Goldstein was pretty rough, although the class wasn't that difficult. He could have lightened up a bit. It was just math, for God's sake. Gastronomy was a little dif-ficult. Studying food and how people eat was much more intricate than I thought. It had a lot to do with biology and how the human body reacts to different foods in differ-ent combinations. Tom and Karen seemed to have a much harder time with everything than I did. Some nights the three of us studied together back at Karen's dorm, but the two of them did more joking around than work. One night before finals in Karen's room, she was on the phone half the time and Tom just threw her stuffed teddy bear up and down over and over again.

"We should party tomorrow night," he said as he caught the bear. "What do you think Jack, party tomorrow after finals?"

"Yeah, I'm in, where to?" I asked eagerly. Partying was kind of my thing at that point, and I hadn't really hung out with anyone from school outside of class, well, outside of small study sessions that is.

"I don't know, we'll just go across the street to that bar—hey Karen, what's the name of that bar across the street we were at the other night?"

"Shenanigans. Why, you wanna go get a drink?"

"Not now, we got to study, I'm talking about after the final tomorrow," Tom replied.

"You sure you don't wanna go now? Molly's going over there in like half an hour. We'll just go for one and then come back here and finish up studying," she said excitedly. "Jack, you wanna go, Molly's going." She started laughing into the phone. The sound of her laugh brought a smile to my face, even though I had no idea why she was laughing.

"Come on boys, let's go. One drink. You think you can handle that ladies, or do you have to study?" she said, talking like a baby and making fun of us.

"All right I'll go, even though I know what your definition of one drink is," Tom said, standing up and stretching.

She looked in my direction. "I'm down," I said without hesitation.

"Molly, let me comb my hair and I'll meet you there, OK? Bye." She hung up the phone and stood up. "One drink guys, then it's back to the books."

The only flaw in this plan was that I was only 17. I don't think they knew that. Karen was 22 and Tom was 23. They'd ask for my ID and then the plan would go straight to hell.

We walked over to the bar. The place wasn't that busy; it was primarily a college bar, and most students had big exams the next day. It was a typical college bar (not that I knew what typical was, then). The wood paneled walls were decorated with posters of different beers. In each corner there were pool tables, and a long wood bar wrapped around two of the walls with long mirrors advertising Guinness Beer behind them. A sunken dance floor off to the left side looked like it could hold a lot of people. It was dimly lit, full of smoke and loud with music from the juke. It seemed like a place I could get used to. Even though I was partying quite a bit, I hadn't been to many bars before, I was always worried that I couldn't get in.

"Hey Tommy, what's up?" the bartender asked.

"Not much, I'm surprised you remember my name."

"Well, you know, guys like you are hard to forget."

"That's true."

Tom was talking to the tall, blonde, sexy bartender. I leaned in and smiled as Tom introduced her to me.

"Christine, you remember my girlfriend Karen, right? And this is Jack Cahill, he's a friend of ours, we're meeting Molly here in about ten minutes," he said winking at the bartender.

"It's nice to meet you Jack. Are you 21?"

"Nope. I'm 23." I figured if I was going to push the envelope here I might as well go all the way.

"Well guys, what'll it be?" she asked without hesitation. If I'd known it was that easy I would have been out more often.

"We'll take two Heinekens, and whatever Jack's having."

"Heineken is fine."

"Three Heine's coming up," she said cheerfully. She turned to the cooler and bent down to get our beers. I saw Tom leaning over the bar to get a good look at her ass. I looked too, but my girl wasn't sitting right next to me, his was. Karen didn't notice though, she was busy watching the door for Molly. The bartender dropped off our beers and smiled at Tom. When she left, Tom tipped his beer in my direction and gave me a wink. Then he sat down next to Karen, put his arm around her, and gave her a kiss on the cheek. The two of them looked over at me, smiling like they had something to say.

"What's up?" I asked smirking.

"Nothing man, you ready for the test tomorrow?" Tommy asked sarcastically.

Karen jumped in, "You know Jack, Molly's ready. She never needs to study for anything, she's one of those people who understand it all the first time they hear it. Are you one of those people Jack?"

"Depends on whether or not I like what I hearing."

"Molly wants you, bro," Tom said, chuckling. Karen smacked him in the arm before he even finished his sentence.

"That's not true . . . I mean, it is true but — OH! Tom you are such a moron!" Karen was tripping over her own words and Tom was laughing hysterically. Karen's face went beet red; you could tell that wasn't how she would have put it. "Jack, I don't know if she 'wants you,' but she does like you. If big mouth could have shut up for a minute, I would have said it with a little more class than he did." She gave him a look of half anger and half love.

"What babe? She likes him, she wants him, is there really much of a difference?" Tom said confidently.

"Quiet down for a second Tom. Jack, what do you think of that?"

"I think I'll keep it in mind," I said, smiling and nodding. It was cool to me that this was happening so soon. Less than a month at school and I was out at a bar, with the hottest girl in class, my new buddy, and a girl who liked me. "Yup, I definitely will keep that in mind," I repeated, still nodding.

"Excuse me," Karen stood up and walked to the door. Molly had walked in and she was racing toward her. They hugged, happy as ever. Karen started whispering into her ear. She got all excited and the two of them walked toward the restrooms laughing. As they walked past us Molly said, "Evening boys, excuse us for a minute." Karen was pulling her arm away from us. They left and walked into the women's room. Tom looked over at me and slapped my knee.

"You got any singles for the jukebox?" he asked.

"Sure, let's go," I said.

At the juke Tom tried to drop some knowledge about the whole Molly thing, truthfully I wasn't really listening to him. I played along and both heeded and humored his advice. As friendly as we were and as mildly interested as I was about the news about Molly, I mostly was just looking over my shoulder to see when Karen would come back. I had no real agenda; things were always just a little more exciting to me when she was around.

"Did you miss us?" Karen asked, grabbing her beer and sitting down next to us.

"Yeah we did, but we got by," Tom said, kissing Karen.

"Hi Jack, how are you tonight?" Molly said, giving me a hug.

"I'm better now that you're here." I said playfully flirting and hugging her back.

"That's good to hear. I can see the studying is going really well," Molly said ordering a beer.

"Well, some of us don't remember everything the first time we hear it." I said sipping my Heineken.

"And some of us do, Jack Cahill. Some of us remember very well." She grinned at me with those chubby cheeks.

The night didn't end after that first drink, in fact the four of us really lived it up. Drinks were flowing non-stop and we all had such a great conversation about everything in our lives. We really got to know each other, where we were from, why we were here, our goals, ambitions, anything and everything. We really bonded, sipping beer and doing the occasional shot. Molly always wanted something light, like a cosmo shot or kamikaze, but Karen could really drink, she wanted whiskey or tequila straight up. Her face always puckered in the cutest way after she would do one, then she would let out a "Woo!" and laugh at herself. She was so much fun and had an amazing sense of humor. Listening to her talk was so easy, in fact too easy. I would sit up and pay full attention, I had to force myself to act distracted occasionally so Tom wouldn't catch me gazing. Conversely Tom paid almost no attention, his eyes were easily averted with almost any girl that walked by, after awhile, he almost looked bored and asked me to shoot some pool. I was a good pool player so I gladly accepted, plus I needed an excuse to get up and stop eyeing Karen from across the table.

Tom and I played pool for hours, looser always bought shots and Tom was even better then I was. I was competitive, but he always found a way to win so needless to say I bought a lot of shots.

The girls chatted at the bar while we played, sipping cold beers and laughing out loud. They were constantly looking in our direction, and I knew I was the topic of their conversation. I loved that they were talking about me. The mood was great all night, though as it went on, Tom started to get pretty drunk. He started busting my chops about Molly; even in front of her he made cracks. He was also getting a little obnoxious with Karen, making rude comments like, "Hey babe, we've talked enough tonight," or, "We gotta hit the books, or maybe your bed babe!" laughing louder after each statement. He was slurring and really tipsy.

"I'm gonna keep this guy to myself if you ladies don't mind," I said, putting my arm around Tom. He was so drunk that I was holding him up. I knew it was time for him to go.

"Oh well Jack, looks like we'll have to get by without him," Molly said, looking me in the eye. She and Karen looked at each other, almost relieved. As she said that, Tom slipped off my arm and fell down.

"All right, we're out of here big guy. Good night ladies, we'll see you tomorrow," I replied hoisting him up. I was bumming because the night was so much fun but someone needed to get him home. Tom hadn't drunk any more than me but he was totally annihilated. He managed to stumble outside on his own accord.

As I followed him out the door, Karen raced up behind me and grabbed the back of my shirt. I didn't really feel it because I was wearing a lot of layers. I always wore layers because I was a skinny guy so I bulked up on layers of clothes. Grabbing me she said, "You're taking Tom home, right Jack?" Her arms were fidgeting between her hips and her chest.

"Well, I was going to; he's not doing very well."

"I know, he always gets this way. He has no tolerance for alcohol. Every time he drinks it's the same thing, he always . . ." She stopped herself short. "Will you do me a favor Jack?"

"Anything Karen, you name it."

"After you take him home, will you come back and tell me how he is?" She put her hand on my shoulder. I looked at it and she saw me take notice.

"Yeah, you bet I will. I'll make sure he gets home safe."

"Good Jack, you do that, and then you come back here. I just, well, I just want to make sure he's ok." she said taking her hand off me but looking me in the eyes. She looked amazing standing there in the dim light.

"Of course." I said. I smiled at her and she smiled back.

Tom was waiting for me outside. He was standing upright and seemed to be doing better now that the fresh air had hit him. He stood still as I approached him.

"So, what do you want to do bro?" I asked him hesitantly.

"Honestly, I would kill to smoke a joint right now," Tommy said, swaying a bit.

"I can arrange that," I said proudly.

"You . . . you have pot?" Tom responded with surprise.

"Yeah bro, you wanna smoke, we smoke."

"Cool man, that's good to know," Tom staggered around a bit. "You know, everyone in our class smokes. In fact, our whole damn industry gets fucked up one way or another every night. You being from the area, and knowing people and stuff, you would be a handy guy to know for a lot of people, maybe even make some money. Look at it this way; you wouldn't have to work at that shitty pizza place anymore, what's it called again, Padrino's? Do you know what Padrino means in Italian? Godfather, that's what it means, you can't get any more generic than that. Think about it guy, that place sucks, no offense or anything." He was spewing nonsense and becoming annoying. I figured if we smoked it might be the last nail in his coffin so he'd pass out and I could get back to the girls. I got a funny vibe that Karen might be interested in more then just a status report on Tom.

"None taken," I responded glumly, barely listening.

Tommy and I finished smoking that joint, he got even more wasted than he was before. He started talking about other girls he'd slept with, and cocaine parties he'd been to, weed was like truth serum to him. He went on and on, I liked some of his stories, but mainly I was itching to be rid of him and get back to the bar.

"Yo Jack, I need to get home. I told you one drink is never one with Karen," he said drunkenly, I think that joint really messed him up.

"You were right bro. We still have a final tomorrow; you need to rest up for it. Karen will be back soon, don't worry about that. I'll get her back here for you—you have my word on that," I said.

"Thanks man, it's good to have a friend like you," he said tiredly.

"It's no problem partner," I said getting him into the car.

I drove Tommy home and helped him to his dorm room. He feel into his bed like a bag of bricks and instantly passed out. Once he did, I raced to my 1987 Nissan Maxima, jumped in, turned up the music, and floored it.

I must have taken a while getting high and talking with Tom because before I knew it, it was almost midnight. We had been out drinking since 6:30. I had a good buzz going when I got back to the bar. There were a lot more people in there now; the parking lot was full corner-to-corner. The music was so loud I could hear it from my car. I checked my hair in the rear view, adjusted my collar, and headed inside.

The bar was packed, standing room only and barely even room for that. I looked around for Karen and Molly but I didn't see them at first. I walked up to the bar and saw Christine, the bartender, and she noticed me right away. She walked over to me.

"Where'd Tommy go?" she yelled over the music.

"He got tired, I just took him home."

"That's sweet of you; tell him I said thanks for saying goodbye when you see him."

"I'll make sure he gets the message," I said, still looking around for the girls.

"Your friends are around the corner playing pool. You want another beer Jack?" she said smiling.

"Yeah, I'd love one." She grabbed me a Heineken and popped the top off. "Thank you," I said. I dropped a nice tip on the bar and headed around the corner. Molly was arm in arm with another guy from class. As soon as I made eye contact with Karen she tapped Molly on the back and signaled in my direction. She broke loose and the two of them smiled at me.

"I didn't think you were coming back," Karen said, walking over to me and standing up straight.

"Well, I made you a promise that I intended to keep. I just dropped Tom off. He's fine, a little drunk, but he's fine."

"Thanks Jack, it's nice of you to look out for him like that. He just can't hold his liquor. Sweet guy, but can't drink to save his life. Every time he opens a beer he doesn't stop until he's drunk," she said.

"Funny, he said the same thing about you," I responded.

"He would," she replied sadly, shaking her head.

"Well, anyway, that's none of my business. I just wanted to tell you he's home safe. I should get going."

"Wait! You should stay, Molly really wants to have a drink with you," she said looking right at me. She had the most perfect blue eyes.

"I don't really want to have a drink with Molly right now," I said swallowing. I couldn't look anywhere but straight into those eyes. I had to go before I said something that might get me into trouble. As I turned to leave, Karen grabbed my hand and I turned back around.

"Do you want to have a drink with me?" she asked, holding my hand. She was gazing straight at me, swinging my arm.

"Well, I'd have to be a fool to pass that up, now wouldn't I?"

"Pretty much," she said, smiling at me. "Stay here for a second, I'll be right back."

She turned and skipped over toward Molly. She whispered something in her ear, grabbed her purse, and headed back over to me. Molly smiled and blew me a kiss. I acted like I grabbed it in mid-air and slapped it on my cheek. She laughed as Karen came back over to me. "Let's take a seat over there." Molly waved as we left.

We walked to the other side of the bar and took a seat at a little round table. I pulled her chair out for her as we sat and she thanked me, still smiling. It was almost as if she never took that beautiful smile off her face. She was absolutely mesmerizing. We started talking and didn't stop for hours. It was late but neither of us seemed to mind. We talked about everything, much like before but this time it was just the two of us so it was much more personal. Our conversation was amazing; we didn't have any awkward pauses the whole time, it just flowed. Every time one person would stop talking and the other would start, it was like the other still wasn't done. I remember telling her about my life's goals which were changing by the minute.

"So, why did you pick this school?" she said curiously.

"Well, I guess that's a long story."

"I'm not going anywhere," she said inquiringly.

"I've been working in restaurants for a couple of years now. I was never really good at anything I'd tried before that. I mean, I was good, but nothing seemed to come as naturally as cooking. I think I have a knack for it or something. Anyway, when I was young, I never had big aspirations in life; I would have been content being a Chef and making a living, but now, at least as of lately . . ."

"What?" she said, hanging on every word I was saying.

"Now . . . now I want to be big. I want to be really big, like name-in-lights kind of stuff. I work with these guys at my restaurant who think they're like rock stars because they can cook, but they're not. They are totally content with what they are doing that they don't have any focus or drive to be something more. The older I get, the bigger the world seems, and the smaller Pleasant Valley, New York gets. I can't be like those guys and just get by, I have to be huge." I sat up straight. I was looking her in the eye the whole time. She was so interested in what I was saying she didn't even realize that I had finished. She just looked at me, nodding.

"I guess that sounds a little self-centered and cocky. I'm sorry," I said sipping my beer.

"You have nothing to be sorry for. You're right, the older we get the smaller our lives seem to get. I've heard a lot of people talk to me about themselves, heard a lot of bullshit about where they think they're going in life, but you . . .you speak with such confidence behind every word you say. I believe you Jack Cahill; I can already see your name in lights."

"Thank you Karen, that means more than you could possibly know coming from you. I mean that. It's nice to have someone like you on my side."

She touched my hand slightly, and as she did, I grabbed her fingers. We were looking each other in the eyes. I started having flashbacks of dropping Tom off at his dorm and how he was my buddy. I gave him my word that I would get her home safely and alone. I wanted to kiss her so bad, and I think she wanted me to, but I couldn't betray my friend, even though I knew he was bad for her. He was always talking to and about other girls around her. She was the sweetest thing in the world; she didn't deserve that. I had feelings inside me that made the ones I had for anyone else before feel like nothing. We just gazed at each other for a second before she said, "Can you take me home Jack?" She was still holding my hand. Her tone was so appealing, and I couldn't say no.

"Yeah, sure I can hon, let's go." *Hon? What am I doing here?*

"Let me just say goodbye," she said, grabbing her purse. "Wait here one sec, OK?" She stared at me all the way down the bar. My heart was racing a mile a minute. This was a once in a lifetime chance here. Was I really going to blow it for some guy I'd met less than a month ago? He was going to find out about this. Karen and had been sitting together all night. He knew the bartender, some classmates were there and now she was telling people we were leaving together. I couldn't do anything, despite how much I liked this girl; he'd kill me.

"You ready to go Jack?"

"Yup, let's go."

We walked outside. I couldn't believe how late it had gotten; it was almost 2am. We had a final in a few hours.

As we walked toward my car, I headed to the passenger side to open the door for her. I tried to get out of her way to go around to the driver's side, but it was a tight squeeze. As I maneuvered around she touched my chest and looked up at me. It was a very sexy look; she was blinking her eyes and swaying slightly. I knew what she wanted.

"You know Jack, not too many guys I know open doors and pull out chairs anymore." She was moving her hand around now.

"Now I'm sure that's not true. I bet guys would bend over backwards just for a chance to speak with you."

"No, it's true. You don't swear, you stand up every time I get up, you ordered me every drink, you're like a perfect gentleman." I was smiling right back at her. My heart calmed down, my palms weren't sweaty anymore, and nobody else mattered. This felt right to me. "So would you have bent over backwards if I asked you to?"

"Me?"

"Yeah you."

"Me huh . . . I think I would have hijacked a space shuttle, launched it, jumped out around the moon, dove back to Earth, and landed in the Pacific. Then I would have swum back to Shenanigans, pulled out your chair, and *then* bent over backwards if that's what it would have taken."

She started laughing out loud. "That's all?" she said, still laughing.

"I'm serious Karen, I'm hooked," I said leaning in toward her.

"What about Molly?"

"I'm not interested in Molly."

"What about Tom?" she asked.

"I'm not interested in him either," I said smoothly.

"Kiss me," she said seriously.

I grabbed her by the back of her head and pulled her up to me. Just before our lips touched I heard her say, "Oh my." That was the last thing she said for about half an hour. We just stood there with my car door open in the middle of the Shenanigans parking lot, kissing. It was the most amazing kiss I have ever had, our hands drifted up and down each other but not to aggressively, it was more passionate and had a very deep feeling to it. When it was over we looked at one another, gently touching and just enjoying each other's company. It was silent, but it was as if the air was full of our thoughts. Karen pulled me closer and finally spoke.

"So what's next?" she asked, holding me around the waist and looking me directly into my eyes.

"Tomorrow," I responded, holding her right back.

"Yeah, tomorrow, we always have tomorrow," she said squeezing me tighter.

"Let me take you home now," I said loosening my grip a little. "Tomorrow's gonna be a big day."

As we drove she held my hand the whole way. We were listening to some slow song on the radio. She wasn't just holding my hand; she was rubbing up and down my arm, looking at me and smiling the entire ride. We didn't speak much, we just kind of stared at each other, breathing happily, and smiling. I was amazed by what was happening to me in that moment, nothing had ever felt like this before.

As we pulled up to her dorm, we parked for a minute. We rubbed each other's arms, gazing at one another for a bit. We still didn't speak, but as she opened the door, I leaned over to kiss her again. She kissed me back for a minute or two. When it was over, she pulled back and smiled at me one last time. She slowly let go of my hand, stepped out of the car and said one word, "Tomorrow."

"Tomorrow," I said as she closed the door. She stretched as she walked to her dorm; I watched her walk the whole way never taking my eyes off her, not even for a second. She turned and looked at me one more time, waved, and went inside. As much as I didn't want the night to end, I'm glad that it did. I liked her, a lot actually and I was happy that such an incredible night was ending so perfectly.

"Wow," I whispered aloud as she disappeared into her building. Stunned, shocked and totally infatuated, I put the car into first gear, and drove away.

CHAPTER 3

KNOCK KNOCK

I got to class about ten minutes early the next day. As I walked into the classroom everyone was seated as normal. My chair was empty of course and Molly and Karen were sitting right behind us as they always did. I approached my seat. Tom pulled it out for me and asked, "You ready for this one bro?"

"Ready for what?" I asked nervously.

"Ready for the test, you jackass? What's with you?" He seemed edgy but I think he was just a little hungover.

"I guess I'm as ready as I'll ever be," I said, taking a deep breath and sitting down. I nodded at the girls as I sat. Karen smiled at me, blushing a bit. I blushed too I guess— she was amazing.

"Hey man," he said, "we had a good time last night huh?" He leaned in toward me still smelling faintly of beer.

"Yeah, it was pretty good," I said, shrugging my shoulders.

"Good luck on this test guys," Molly said, patting us on the backs. I turned around to thank her and sneak another look at Karen. She was shaking her head and biting her lower lip as Molly was glancing in my direction. I turned back around to Tom.

"So, did you hook up last night?" he whispered to me.

"What?" I yelped. I knocked my books off the table. The whole class looked over at me for a second.

"I mean with Molly, man. You OK?" he asked, looking at me funny.

"Yeah, I'm all right," I responded picking up my books.

He leaned back in toward me. "So did you or not?" he asked again. As he did, Mr. Goldstein walked into class. We both sat up straight. I thought Tom gave me a look as we leaned back, almost as if he knew I was acting suspicious. Mr. Goldstein started talking about the final and we all listened. This was the first big test of our college careers. As he was handing out the tests, I snuck a peek back towards Karen. She was looking up toward the teacher. As she saw me looking she winked at me and whispered "good luck" under her breath. She smiled and looked back up. I turned around and focused on the test.

The whole thing took me less than an hour; I was in and out of there. I put my pen down, dropped my test on Mr. Goldstein's desk, shook his hand and left. As I left, I looked over toward Karen but she was very engrossed in her test. I closed the door and walked out.

Walking down the hallway I heard the door close behind me. It was a classmate of mine, Brad Taylor, who seemed to be an all right guy. "Hey Cahill, wait up," he called.

"Hey Brad, how did you do?"

He smirked. "That thing was a joke, I took harder math tests in second grade," he said, still stuffing his books back into his bag.

"Yeah really," I chuckled. It was a really easy final.

"So I'm having some people over at my place tonight if you want to come?" Brad said.

"Yeah, that'd be cool. What time?" I asked.

"Whenever is good for you. Oh and Cahill, ask those girls Karen and Molly if they want to come too. They're friends of yours, right? I hear Molly's got a thing for you, eh?" he asked, elbowing me in the arm.

"They're friends; I'll make sure I tell them, Brad."

He took off around the corner. With hours to kill before the party, I headed back to my house, stopping off at Padrino's to check my schedule for following week. I had become a strong cook there, able to work any station and handle it with ease. Where before it felt like pressure, now it had become routine. I had become so used to the volume and stress of a busy kitchen that now Chris was depending on me for leadership in his absence. I was honored, but I was also quickly distracted with school and my desire for bigger things. I chit chatted with Chris and the crew for a few minutes, stopped at home to get dressed and headed to Brad's.

As planned, I hit the party at 8:30. I found Brad's apartment with no problem. The music was loud and I could hear people yelling and laughing from two floors down. It sounded like a good party. I walked up the front steps, rubbing my hands together, and opened the front door.

"Cahill! Hey Cahill's here!" Brad screamed as he opened the door for me.

"Cahill!" People screamed as I came in. My whole class was at Brad's house.

I gave a wave to the crowd. It was a cool party. The room I walked into was totally cleared out for a beer pong table. The only other thing in that room was a stereo system playing some classic rock. "Come on Cahill, let's get you a beer."

Brad and I walked through his apartment. It had wood floors, low ceilings, and was a little run-down. He had nice stuff though, and he seemed to know how to throw a party.

"You want a beer? A shot? What do you want, Cahill?" He always called everyone by their last names.

"Both," I said.

He laughed and poured me one of each. "Cheers," he said, tipping his cup to me. "Karen and Molly are coming, right, Cahill?"

"I never asked 'em, I forgot," I apologized.

"Don't worry man; Tommy's coming over in a bit. I'm sure they'll come with him."

"If he's coming, they'll be here," I replied derisively. He headed around the corner to a cute little short-haired blonde and gave her a kiss. I stood near the keg and hustled to finish my first one. It looked like I had some catching up to do.

"Hey Cahill," Brad said. "This is my girlfriend Emma, say hello honey." He dipped her backwards and laughed hysterically.

"Hey Cahill!" she screamed. "Nice ta meet ya!" she said, standing up straight.

"It's nice to meet you too Emma," I said with a smile. She giggled, waving at me as she and Brad walked over toward the beer pong table. I made some conversation with a few people from class, small talk about professors, the final, I even played a quick game of beer pong and lost, but I was really looking out for Karen and Molly to show up.

Oh, and Tommy too. I hadn't even had an opportunity to speak with them about the test today. I was really hoping to feel him out about last night.

I headed back to the kitchen for another beer and when I returned, I saw Karen and Molly hugging and kissing people as they walked through the door. Tommy walked right past the girls as they were saying their hellos and came over to me. "So, I only have one question for you Jack." He looked me in the eye with a serious grin on his face. My heart almost beat out of my chest. "Are we goanna let Brad stay on this beer pong table all night, or are we gonna beat his ass?"

"I'd like to see you try, big boy," Brad said, hitting another shot.

"Jack and I are up next my friend, it's not gonna be pretty for you," Tom boasted.

"We'll see man, we'll see," Brad replied, winking at him and laughing.

Tommy turned back to me. "I've got to get a beer man, you want one?"

"No, I just grabbed one."

"Go say hello to Molly man, she was talking about you on the ride over," he said quietly, not moving his lips too much. He must have had no idea about Karen and me.

"All right, I will, beer's right around the corner in the kitchen, bro." I took a deep breath of relief.

"Thanks," he said, slapping me on the back as he went by. Karen was looking in my direction and smiling. She gave a little wave from across the room. She looked sensational, wearing gray wool pants and a tight navy blue short-sleeve shirt that was hanging on her shoulders right where her perfect brown hair met it. I nodded and gave a wink. She was saying hello to Brad and meeting his girlfriend so I didn't want to interrupt. She kept looking over her shoulder at me the whole time though, rocking back and forth on the balls of her feet and smiling. I just watched happily.

"So, we on the table yet?" Tom asked, returning from the kitchen.

"Excuse me one second," Brad said to Emma and Karen. He picked up a ball and threw it into the last cup on the other side of the table. "You are now and you're in trouble, too. I already played Cahill tonight, he didn't do so well, isn't that right Cahill?" He spoke with a Pennsylvania accent, laughing the whole time he was talking trash. He was a great guy.

"Don't worry Brad, I was just warming up," I replied cracking my knuckles. "I won't be such a pushover this time."

"Let's do it," Tommy said, lining up his cups.

Karen, Molly, and Emma walked over to the kitchen to get some drinks. "Hiiiii Jack," Karen and Molly said, waving as they passed by and left the room.

"Hi ladies," I said, waving back and getting ready to play. I really wanted to talk with Karen, but it was best if I just laid low for a bit. The guys were ready to play.

For all the trash talking Tom was doing, he sure didn't back it up. He only hit two shots the whole time; I made eight myself, but our efforts fell short as Brad and his partner John made mincemeat out of us. The whole game lasted four minutes.

"He's got the home court advantage here, I wasn't used to the bounce of the table that game, we have to play again," Tom said, stuttering with frustration. He didn't like to lose.

"Excuses, excuses, now get back in line and I'll see you chumps in a few games," Brad said cockily.

"All right, we'll be back," Tom said, trying to hide his disappointment. We went to the kitchen to grab some more brews and found the girls sitting there with a few other people, having a drink. The place was filling up; there must have been about 40 people in that little apartment.

As we walked in, Molly stood up and gave me a hug. "I was wondering when you were gonna say hello, Mr. Cahill."

"How are you Mol?" I asked, kissing her on the cheek.

"Great, how'd you do on the final today?" she asked energetically.

"I did all right, I think."

"Well you better have, you were like, the first one out of there."

"Well, I either know something or I don't, staring at a piece of paper has never given me an answer before."

"Unless there was a pretty girl's number on it," she said, laughing and elbowing me in the side. Karen glanced up at me.

"Well, I suppose if I ever got one, I would look at it for a while."

"Oh, I bet you do just fine with the ladies," she said.

"I do what I can."

"How come you don't have a girlfriend Jack?" she asked.

"Yes Jack, why don't you have a girlfriend?" Karen asked trying not to smile. It wasn't bad enough, what I'd done to Tom, but now Karen was making cracks around Molly who she knew liked me. I had to play it cool.

"I guess I just haven't found the right girl yet."

"Yeah, but there's a lot of fun to be had with the wrong ones in the meantime, right, Jack?" Tom decided to chime in.

"You can be a real ass sometimes, Tom," Karen said standing up and looking in my direction. "How much fun have you had with the wrong ones?" she asked, frustrated. The room got quiet.

"I don't know, I'll let you know when I find the right one," he said rudely, sticking his hand out to me for a high five. Karen looked furious and stormed out of the room. Molly looked at me and followed her. I just gave Tommy a look of disappointment. I could tell he was already a little drunk. "What's her problem?" he asked blankly.

"You were a little out of line bro," I said, standing by even though I just wanted to race after Karen.

"It was a joke!" he said loudly. "Oh, you guys know I was kidding, right?" he asked, trying to rally support from the remaining guys in the room. "Jack, you know I was kidding man, how fucking sensitive can she be?"

"Well I know, but maybe she doesn't."

"Fuck her! Oh yeah, I just did that a few hours ago," he said.

"Hey!" I said, pointing my finger in his face and leaning in a bit. "You're out of line, my friend; watch the way you talk about her." I looked him dead in the eye for a second and then stormed out of the room.

The girls were talking near the radio. Molly saw me and flicked her head in my direction, and Karen turned around. She looked a little pissed but she still waved at me. I was really watching every move I made that night. I couldn't let on to anyone about Karen and me, especially Tom, so I was a little hesitant to go right over to the girls.

Karen waved me over in a second or two anyway. She put her arm around me and said, "I think you and I could beat Brad and John, what do you think?" We looked at each other for a second or two and both smiled simultaneously.

"Yeah, I do, I think we can do anything together."

"My drink's empty, I'm going to get another one, I need, I mean, do you guys want one?" Molly said nervously.

"I'd love one Mol," I said, smiling.

"Me too," Karen replied.

"OK. I'll be back in a minute," she said, grabbing our cups from us.

"We'll be here," Karen said looking at me. Molly watched for a second and then dashed away.

Brad found us and said, "Cahill, did I hear Macrillo say you guys could beat us?"

"Yeah, that's right Taylor, we own you next game," Karen said as her eyes lit up.

"This will be over in a second, so get ready lads; I'm just warming up," he said as he was playing his 20th game. He must have drunk a case of beer by himself. When Brad hit the last shot, Karen grabbed my hand and pulled me over to the table. "You're going down Taylor, Jack and I are gonna kick your butt."

The music was loud, there were a lot of people around cheering for each team, and Karen was laughing and giving me high fives after we hit a shot. We played better than any other team that night and finally managed to finally defeat Brad. The place went wild, Karen gave me a huge hug and smile, it was such a fun moment. After we won Molly came around the corner with our drinks. "Tom's gone you guys," she said.

"Gone? He's our ride," Karen said, concerned. Her mood changed quickly.

"I can give you guys a ride," I said.

She looked up at me, "Good, then who needs him. If he's gonna be a jerk I don't want to be with him, either."

"You OK Karen?" Molly asked, putting her arm around her.

"I'm just fine Mol, thank you though."

"You guys want to head out?" I asked.

"It's up to you Mol," Karen said.

"Yeah, let's go, we had a late night last night anyway. I could use a good night's rest after this month, you know."

On our way out, Brad razzed us a bit about winning and walking but the girls explained that they were tired so he gave them a kiss on the cheek as they walked out the door. I went to shake his hand and he said, "You owe me a rematch Cahill."

"Looking forward to it brother."

Karen and Molly were waiting for me outside. We hopped into my car and drove towards campus. The moment was damn near perfect. I had Karen in my car again only this time she and Tom were fighting and were possibly finished. Molly was also there, so I had to drop her off first. We pulled up in front of Molly's dorm at 1am; she gave me a kiss on the cheek and said goodnight to us. As she walked to her dorm she smiled and waved me to come upstairs. I just waved back, shook my head, and drove away.

Karen grabbed my hand and rolled her eyes onto me. "You want to come upstairs tonight to talk, maybe have a glass of wine? I've got a great bottle of Chardonnay that my parents bought me. You'll love it."

"I would like nothing more," I said with feeling.

"Great, you can park right over there near that bench."

We walked up to her room, where the whole thing started the night before; who knew that studying for a final could lead to all this. When the door closed she turned off the lights and threw her arms around me. She hugged me for a minute or so and then started kissing me. Again I wasn't nervous, my heart was beating fast, but kissing her just felt so right. "So how 'bout some of that wine Jack, I'd say you've earned it," she asked me, lips to lips.

"I'll get the glasses," I said smoothly.

"Who said anything about glasses?" She said seductively. She started kissing me again, more passionately than before.

BOOM, BOOM, BOOM! "Karen, you in there?" It was Tom, banging on the door. We looked at each other in shock.

"Uh, yeah, but um, I'm on the phone, and what do you want anyway Tom," she said startled.

"I just want to talk. I was out of line before at the party and I wanted to say I'm sorry. Can I come in?" Karen closed her eyes tight to think.

"No, but when I'm off the phone I'll come over to your room." I looked at her in disbelief.

"Fair enough, thank you Karen, I'll see you when you get there babe." We heard him walk away.

"You're not actually going are you?" I asked, extremely confused at that point.

"If I didn't say that he would have never left, and if I don't go he'll be back. Either way he'll know you're here. Why don't you just wait here for ten minutes or so while I go get rid of him and I'll be right back? Then we can have that wine," she said, kissing my lower lip.

"That sounds like a date," I said, calming down and smiling. Of course she'd be right back, she liked me.

"I'll see you in a few, make yourself comfortable," she said, blowing me a kiss as she walked out the door.

Ten minutes passed and she wasn't back. Twenty, and still nothing. A half hour later I started getting pretty tired. To stay awake I opened the bottle of Chardonnay. After a whole hour had gone by and she still hadn't returned, the wine was gone. I kept saying, "Five more minutes and I'm out of here." I think I said it 15 times.

Eventually, when my blood was boiling, I stood up, a little drunk from the bottle of wine, and took off. I couldn't believe Karen would do that to me. *What the hell did they have to talk about, he always treated her with no respect, and she said she'd had enough of him.* It seemed pretty open and shut to me. I was pissed. I stood up to Tom for her, and like that I was left in limbo. *The hell with this, I'm out of here.* I walked outside and just stood there for a minute looking up to the sky for an answer, and then it hit me.

Knock, knock, knock. It was 2:30am.

"Well Mr. Cahill, I was hoping you'd come over." Molly opened the door wearing her nightgown. She looked really good just then. "What took you so long?"

"Like I said, great things are worth waiting for." She put her arms around me and closed the door.

CHAPTER 4

WELCOME ABOARD

Months later I still had very strong feelings for Karen, but she and Tom had apparently gotten back together. After she heard that Molly and I slept together the two of us kind of cooled off. We were both a little hurt but maybe we were just a fleeting glimpse and even though we wanted it, the timing was all wrong. It was probably for the best though; school was getting much more difficult, and we were all focused more on work. The chefs became tougher and the work was almost overwhelming sometimes.

We were in full-time kitchens at this point and I was quickly rising to the top of my class. I aced my classes, and the chefs were very impressed by my ability to understand the cooking methods so rapidly. My skills were smooth but my tactics were a little unconventional; some people called me a cowboy cook. Every time we had a class competition on speed or accuracy I was the first to turn in my plate and my chef was always impressed with the quality and accuracy. There was pressure, big pressure not only to perform in class but to perform socially. This environment demanded you work well with others, form bonds, and maintain them with their due respect. It's an industry where contacts matter; who you know is almost as important as what you know, so forging firm bonds with other strong cooks is imperative.

It wasn't always so easy. Chef Wolf screamed at me for failing to drizzle butter on top of my sauce béchamel, because when you don't it forms a crust on top, like skin on pudding. He blasted me in front of the whole class, despite praising my other sauces. It was that type of place—chefs, especially the old European ones, didn't hold back. If you made a mistake they had no problem letting you know publically in a loud, embarrassing tone. Maybe that was their way of teaching or maybe they just enjoyed the power. Time was flying, and before I could turn around and blink we were going off to our externships.

Karen talked about going to Delaware to be near her family; she had a tight bond with them and missed being close to home. Molly was going to Vegas and Tom didn't have a site; I'm not even sure he left the Hudson Valley at all. As for myself, I wanted more. I also had to get the hell out of the mess I'd created with the drama of Karen and Tom, sleeping with Molly, all of it. I'd always wanted to work in Chicago or Las Vegas, but mainly I wanted to be in the center of the universe, New York City, the restaurant capital of the world. I thought it would be a great place to lose myself for a bit and just clean my head out. New York had some of the most well respected restaurants on the planet. I felt drawn to it and that's where I needed to be. After a couple of weeks spent evaluating which restaurant was best suited for me, I decided to go with The Dexter House on the corner of 59th Street and 9th Avenue. It was one of the most prestigious restaurants in New York at the time, I was lucky to be accepted.

Chef Michael Roderick was an accredited graduate of the CIA, with numerous awards. He was about six feet tall with a thick red beard and a strong build. He was also a complete womanizer with a suave way about him, and he always had a different girl, but he was one hell of a serious chef. I met him for the first time in the spring of 1997.

This was my first real trip to New York City. I was born in Long Island, and had plenty of family from New York City, but I'd never really gone there on my own. The Dexter House didn't look like much when I first saw it—in fact, I drove right past it a couple of times on my first visit—but when I went inside I was blown away by the atmosphere.

The bar was sleek, in a half oval shape along the east wall, and illuminated from behind with classic white lighting. Large crystal chandeliers hung from the 20-foot high ceiling along the main strip of tables, which all had thick white tablecloths and real silver pre-set. There were 250 seats in the restaurant and a large presidential-style podium at the front door. It had multiple elevations, some carpeted and others with well-kept hardwood floors. It was spacious without being cavernous. When I entered, a man wearing a well-tailored navy pinstriped suit and too much cologne greeted me with a thick accent: "Welcome to the Dexter House sir, how can I be of service to you?"

"I'm here to see Chef Michael," I responded politely. I wasn't looking too bad myself, wearing a nice black suit and tan tie.

"Who should I say is here sir?" he asked.

"Jack Cahill," I responded confidently. He nodded, turned, and walked towards the back of the restaurant.

I stood patiently for about two minutes; there was plenty to look at. The place was absolutely beautiful, very old New York but modernized. Chef Mike came around the corner, walking quickly. "Jack Cahill I presume, Mike Roderick, nice to meet you, let's take a seat over here," he pointed toward a table in the corner.

I started talking on the way there, "Chef let me just start out by saying what a great honor it is to—"

Mike interrupted, "You can skip the bullshit kid; we don't take that many interns here so listen up. I spoke to a few of your chefs from school and they all say you have great skills and you're a quick learner, but they also say your approach isn't always by the book. Here we do it all by the book, there's no room for cowboys who think they're the best thing since sliced bread, you got me? We don't make mistakes and we're not about to start with you, is that clear young man?"

"Yes chef!" I replied militaristically.

"Good." He took a breath and said, "Take a seat. We accepted you because your references all say you have what it takes to be a great chef. Here you will listen. You will listen and learn. There's only one voice that means anything in that kitchen and that's mine. I can help you get ahead quickly, but you will do as I say all day, every day, copy?"

"Yes chef," I repeated.

"You will work here for no money, you will live 20 miles away in housing we will provide, but you are responsible for getting to and from here every day. If you're late you're gone, if you're drunk you're gone, if you fuck up one too many times you are gone, understand?"

"Yes chef, I understand."

"OK Jack, welcome aboard, this is the big time, New York City, The Dexter House, *New York Times* best restaurants four years in a row, 3 Michelin stars, James Beard awards, no time for games here this is as real as it gets. I'll see you tomorrow at 7am, be ready," Mike said, standing up.

"Thank you chef, you won't be sorry."

"Get some rest kid, you're going to need it," he said as he walked away.

As I left I nodded to the guy at the front desk and he signaled me to stop. He handed me an envelope with directions to and from my new apartment. The plans seemed to be nice, but when I got there it was a whole different story.

As I entered the apartment, a large rough neck guy greeted me. He told me the one room apartment had no kitchen, no bathroom, and no tolerance for disturbing the peace. He basically scared the hell out of me.

The apartment was a dump, but it was mine, my first apartment in New York City—although I wasn't sure I was still in New York with the ride I'd just taken. No matter what though, I was determined. I couldn't think about anything back home. After the pep talk by my new chef, I was focused on the job. I had been drinking and smoking a lot, and everything with Karen, it was all stuff I just wanted to wipe away and start over.

I had a hard time falling asleep that night. The apartment was noisy, and my neighbors seemed to stay up even later then I would—but even if they'd been quiet, I still would have been awake. My apartment smelled like a corpse was sleeping in the bed next to me. The only furnishings in the room were a fold-out cot and my suitcase. It was a lonely start, but for me it was perfect.

I stared at the ceiling until 3:30am. I kept picturing the restaurant, and thinking through my game plan for the next day. I wanted to be humble to start; I was the bottom of the barrel but I was sure that I would move right up. I had to be confident; without that, I wouldn't stand a chance. I fell asleep at 4am.

CHAPTER 5

ROASTED EGGPLANT CAVIAR

My apartment was in Queens, and it took about a half hour on the bus to get to work, depending on traffic. I only slept for an hour, but I wasn't tired. I was too excited to be tired. I was heading into my dream job, and even though it was for no money, I knew I was going to learn a lot and hopefully make a few good contacts.

I got to work ten minutes early. It was quiet and all the lights were low, but I could hear the faint sounds of a radio coming from the kitchen. I headed over with my head held high, dressed in my uniform, with my knife kit under my arm. I turned the corner and saw a few guys prepping away, drinking coffee. The kitchen was immaculate. The walls were all stainless steel and so were the countertops. All the equipment was original and well-kept. The grill was spotless and so was the sauté range. It smelled great, like fresh soups and sauces.

"Hi guys, my name is Jack, is Chef Mike in?" I asked them.

They looked at each other and laughed, "Chef's never here this early, he comes in closer to service time," one of them responded. The other one turned to me, "You the new intern?" he asked.

"Yup, what's your name, man?" I asked, extending my hand.

"My name is Craig, and this is Fezzy. We do the prep in the mornings here; you'll be working with us for the next few months." They shook my hand and laughed.

"There must be some mistake, I'm supposed to be working with the chef and cooking, I'm from the CIA," I said proudly. They both laughed out loud at me.

"Welcome to the club, my friend. All you CIA guys prep with us. There are seven cooks here and Chef Mike. They're the only ones who do any cooking around here. You'll be peeling carrots and slicing onions with us prep guys. It's not so bad, the hours suck, but we get all the coffee we want and nobody bothers us. Every so often Chef Mike has us do some special stuff, but for the most part it's pretty routine," Craig explained to me. I just looked confused.

"You want to get started or what, amigo?" Fezzy asked. He was Mexican, I think, with a little mustache and black hair. He spoke with a very strong accent, and was in perfect uniform.

"Yeah might as well, no time like the present," I said, putting my knife kit down and taking out my chef's knife. A chef's knife, or French knife, is a basic ten-inch kitchen blade; it was the only one I ever used. Everyone else had ten different blades for all the different tasks—one for peeling, slicing, boning out meat—but not me, I always used the same one. It was all I needed. Feeling a little embarrassed, I regained my composure and got ready to work. "Nothing wrong with a little prep work, huh guys. Where should I start? Do we have a list?" I asked confidentially.

"We sure do. Every night before Chef goes home he writes us a prep list. It usually takes all day, this restaurant is busy, man," Craig responded. Fezzy didn't seem to say much but he looked like he knew what he was doing in the kitchen. "You can start by making eggplant caviar," he said, glancing at the prep list. "It's easy to make but it takes a while. You have to get two cases of eggplant from the cooler and mince them up. Be careful though, Chef wants it done a certain way, all the cuts have to be perfect 1/8" cuts. If it's too big he'll make you re-cut it."

"No problem." I went over to the cooler to grab the eggplant.

The cooler was huge and very well organized; it smelled so sanitary and clean. All the food was nicely wrapped and the walls and floors shone. Each item had its own clear container that was labeled and dated. Everything had its place; Chef Mike was hyper-organized. Over to the left I saw the eggplant with the rest of the produce. I grabbed it and went back to the line. Craig and Fez were cutting away at 100 pounds of onions. I asked them to show me how to do one eggplant and the rest I could do on my own.

The process was harder than I thought. After they sliced it thin on the slicer machine, they cut all the pieces in half, then cut those into long thin strips, and then cut them into little tiny 1/8" dice, called brunoise. After all the eggplant was cut we soaked it in aged olive oil, garlic, sea salt and white pepper, and then baked it until they all shriveled up and looked like little caviar pieces. They told me the two cases of eggplant cut up would fill eight gallons raw, and two gallons cooked. No problem, or so I thought.

Stepping up to my first task I wanted to impress the guys. I sliced it all in less than 45 minutes, and the actual dicing of it took me about two and a half hours. I seasoned it and got it right into the ovens. Craig and Fezzy were picking fresh herbs by then.

"What's next fellas?" I asked, pleased with my timing.

"You can help us finish up these herbs, man," Craig said.

"Excuse me muchachos," Fezzy turned and left.

I picked some rosemary and parsley for about twenty minutes with Craig, and Fezzy came back over as we finished up. We put everything into containers and put it into the cooler. "You guys want to grab a smoke?" Craig asked, putting a cigarette in his mouth. "Do you smoke Jack?"

"Yeah, is that OK to do?" I replied.

"Sure man, everyone smokes here, let's go outside," Craig said.

We headed out through the back door into an alley with trash sprawled out everywhere. "You got a light?" I asked. I guess people are the same everywhere you go.

Fez lit me up and we got to talking. I told them about Padrino's and the CIA, basic getting-to-know-you stuff. Turned out, Craig was 19 and Fez was 22. They seemed like cool guys. We got along quickly.

We headed back in and got to work. They asked me to hand mince five pounds of fresh garlic, and then do the same to ginger. I told them it wouldn't be a problem as long it wasn't eggplant. As I said that I realized that I'd never taken my eggplant out of the oven. *Oh my God!* It must have been so burnt by that point. I dropped what I was doing and ran over to the oven as fast as I could. My hands were shaking as I ripped open the oven door. It was empty, the stuff was gone! Where the hell was it? I turned around and saw Craig and Fezzy holding back their laughter. When they saw me look at them, they busted out. Fezzy had to lean on Craig he was laughing so hard. "Everything OK Jack?" Craig asked sarcastically.

"Where is it?" I said nervously.

"Where is what Jack?" he replied.

"The caviar! Did it burn?" I ranted.

"It's OK amigo. It's in the cooler safe and sound." Fez said.

"Who took it out?" I asked, taking a deep breath.

"Fezzy did. Don't feel bad, everyone forgets that stuff the first time. Fezzy's an old hand at this, he saved my ass the first time I made it, isn't that right Fez?" Craig asked, patting his chest.

"Absolutely, my friend," Fez answered back. "I saved you and the rest of the CIA," he said, chuckling. "Too bad nobody saved me my first time, Chef was so fucking mad with me that day."

"Thank you Fez," I said.

"We got to watch each other's back around here," Craig said, getting a bit serious. "Everyone watches out for each other. Nobody's above the team here. We might not like the cooks, but we watch their backs; it's the only way to avoid pissing Chef off. If you are going to make it here, look out for the guy next to you before you look out for yourself, trust me man, it will do you a lot of good." He headed off to the cooler as he was finishing speaking.

"He's right," Fezzy turned and followed him. As they left I hunched over and put my hands on my knees to breathe. If I had burned that on my first day I would have been finished. Thank God Fez was looking out for me. I appreciated it, and swore I would do the same for him one day.

The rest of the day was spent chopping garlic and cleaning chicken breasts. The prep team did the bulk stuff that the cooks didn't have time to do. When they came in we had our part done so they could run with our stuff, but also prep their quicker items as well as set up their stations. Prep was all very entry-level, but repeating the simple processes over and over made the motions natural and in itself was great training. The cooks started to come in around 2:00pm. I thought I could compete with any of them, and all I needed was a chance to prove it.

Chef Mike came in around 3:00. He was wearing sunglasses and had a cute blonde on his arm. "See ya tonight Jill," he said, slapping her butt and giving her a kiss goodbye. He slammed the door as she walked out. "Chef Jack, how's the prep?" He asked, looking over my shoulder at Fezzy and Craig. "Oh, these two guys, what did you do all day, eggplant caviar?" he said while taking off his sunglasses.

I looked over at them, "No, Fezzy did that, I focused on several other tasks this morning, they're really good teachers. That stuff looks like it would take me a while to make."

"Did Fezzy get it cut in less than six hours today?"

"One hour boss, one hour," Fezzy shouted from across the room.

"Yeah, one hour my ass, Fezzy, that shit takes you all day," Chef Mike said, putting his sunglasses in his backpack. "Come on CIA, come to my office," he said walking out to the dining room. I followed closely. The guys were laughing at me under their breath.

Chef's office was a real mess. The office itself was clean, but his desk and floor were covered in clothes, shoes, and papers.

"Maid on vacation this week Chef?" I said with a smirk on my face.

"No, I don't have one, but if you want some overtime, the job is yours," he said, smiling at me and changing his shoes. "I got something for you." He flicked his head towards the end of his desk. I pointed to a box and he nodded. I opened up the box and found a chef's jacket with the Dexter House logo on it and my name. "It ought to fit you, you're about my height and build." He looked up as he finished adjusting his shoes.

"Chef, I don't know what to say."

"Well don't say much, it's the only one you're getting for free here so don't get it dirty. You can wear your CIA jacket if you want, but a real chef always has his own restaurant's jackets on. You remember that kid," he said, standing up and fixing his belt.

"I will Chef, and thank you so much, this means a lot to me," I said sincerely. Even though I was thankful I don't think I could have expressed my overwhelming sense of pride. It was my first real coat, like my first badge of honor, wow.

"Great. Now get the hell out of here, your shift's over, come back tomorrow same time, those guys could use the help," Chef said, buttoning up his coat.

"I will sir, thanks again," I said, walking out of the office backwards. I practically tripped while I was at it.

CHAPTER 6

CHEF ON THE LINE!

The weeks in the Big Apple were some of the fastest of my life. Things moved at a totally different pace than I was accustom to, and people were very different than upstate. After getting to know the city, I became very used to the lifestyle but also witnessed a lot of crazy shit there. I saw drunks vomit on the subways, I saw someone who lived in my apartment building get arrested, and I saw a guy kick over a hot dog stand because the guy wouldn't break a fifty dollar bill. There, I quickly learned to mind my own business.

Business at the restaurant was unbelievable. We were full every night we were open. I wasn't doing any actual cooking but I stayed some nights to watch the kitchen run. Chef Mike was amazing; he had full control of the cooks at all times and they all respected him. Chef had taught them all how to prepare some of the world's finest foods and New York's best. They listened to every word he said.

It takes a great leader to make people respect them. It's easy to be feared; all you have to do is threaten or bully people who are weaker than you. Tell people you'll take away their jobs, their income, their stability, and they'll listen to anything you say. But that's not how Chef Mike approached it, even though a lot of chefs did.

Chef Mike was respected because he was there night after night with his guys. He was there first, he'd earned his title, and he never let it get to his head. That's why they loved him, and followed him.

They worked silently all night long. The only voice you heard was Chef's, and on the rare occasion he got upset, he never dealt with it then, it wasn't his style. At the end of the night, he would come over to the cook who'd messed up, whisper in his ear to see him in the office and have a sit-down. After the sit-down, the cook came back to the kitchen and cleaned it all by himself. This didn't happen often, but people had seen it done before.

The hum of the kitchen was the real music to my ears though: orders being called and called back over the volume of a full high-energy dining room, the clanking of sauté pans and the shuffling of silverware, I loved it all.

Something about it just appealed to me and I couldn't get enough.

One early day, Craig, Fezzy and I were scheduled to do prep. I showed up at my usual time and the doors were locked. I looked through the window and all the lights were out. I guessed the guys were running late.

Since they were the only ones with keys besides Chef Mike, I had no choice but to wait. I sat around until 7:30am, but I was getting concerned. They hadn't been late once during the previous two months. I walked over to the payphone and called Craig.

"Hello?" A weak voice answered on the other end.

"Craig, it's Jack, you OK?" I asked, concerned. He sounded awful.

"No man, I'm sick," he replied.

"Well how am I supposed to get into work?" I asked.

"Isn't Fezzy there?"

"No man, he's not here yet either. What should I do?"

"Call Fezzy." He sounded like he was gonna die.

"All right Craig, I'll call him, you get some rest pal, I'll see you soon."

I quickly dialed Fezzy's house and some guy answered who didn't speak any English.

"I needy Fezzy por favor!" I said in the best Spanish I knew.

"Fezzy, uno momento!" he said. I could hear him screaming to Fezzy loudly in the background.

"Hola, que pasa?" he said, obviously fatigued.

"Fezzy, it's Jack, from work," I said.

"Hey Jack man, me no bueno today my friend." Fezzy sounded sick himself.

"You're sick too. Craig isn't coming in either, you sure you guys didn't just drink too much last night?" I asked.

"No man nothing, Craig called out too?" he asked, clearing his throat.

"Yes Fez, he says he's sick, how am I gonna get into the restaurant?" I asked nervously.

"Calm down amigo, I'll call Chef, he'll come let you in, just sit tight for a while OK hombre?"

"OK Fez, call him right away buddy, will ya?" I asked taking a deep breath and looking at my watch. New York sure was busy at 7:30am.

"I call, ciao my friend."

"Bye Fez." I hung up the phone. Nothing to do now but wait. Sitting alone there I had a realization: I was alone. It was the first time I'd noticed. I was alone in the middle of New York City, sitting on the steps of a place where I didn't even get paid, hoping to do the job of three people.

The air was dense, the streets were loud, and the foot traffic was unbelievable. People were racing in this city 24 hours a day. Everyone had something to do every second and I felt like one of them. Inside the walls of the Dexter House I would rock and roll at every given opportunity. I just wanted to get inside and kick some butt.

Hours went by and I smoked about a pack of cigarettes sitting there. Chef Mike showed up around 10:15. He approached me and asked, "Break time already?"

"That's funny, what took you so long?"

"Why did what take me so long?" he asked, taking off his sunglasses and staring at me blankly.

"To get here? Didn't you talk to Craig or Fezzy?" I asked confused.

"No, I didn't. Why would I talk to them?" he said, grinding his teeth and almost looking angry.

"They're not here Chef, I've been waiting here for three hours for you, they said they called you."

"No they didn't. You mean no one is here but you?" he asked aggressively.

"No. But if they didn't call you, why are you here?" I replied curiously.

"Well, Ed can't work tonight either. I need someone to work the line so I was gonna tell Fez he needed to stay, but if he's not here—"

I interrupted, "I'll do it! I mean, I'll do it if you'd like me to, Chef."

"No, you're gonna have your hands full with the prep today, you can't do all that and then set up a station and cook all night, you're not trained or ready for that," he said, unlocking the door. You could see the wheels spinning in his head, he was always calculating and formulating ways to stay progressive, like his mind didn't have an off switch.

"Chef, I know I'm sort of new here, but I can do anything you allow me to. I know you have no reason to, but please trust me. I've been watching the cooks at night and I know the food. Give me a chance and I won't let you down sir," I pleaded, looking him right in the eye.

"Well, with the amount of prep you have to do you're gonna need some help. I like you kid, why don't you and I bang out the prep together and then I'll talk you through the set-up for your station, sound good?" he asked.

"Sounds perfect Chef, let me suit up and I'll meet you on the line in just one minute."

"Take your time Jack, I'm not going anywhere," he said, feeling the edge of the knife he'd just taken out of his bag. It was a Global knife, about 12 inches long and razor sharp.

I got dressed in less than two minutes, put on my hat, grabbed my knife, and hit the line. Chef was a little more professional than Craig and Fezzy, but he seemed to be loosening up around me. "What kind of music do you like?" he asked.

"All kinds I guess," I answered blindly.

"Well, how about this kind," he said, turning up the radio playing some hard rock. "Do you like Metallica?" he asked.

"Sure Chef, I like them fine," I replied coolly.

"I went to see these guys last year at Madison Square Garden. They put on quite a show man."

"I've never seen them live before," I said, sounding inexperienced.

"Well let me tell you Jack, they fucking rock. I took this girl who was working here at the time, her name was Amy, she was 5'9, blonde hair, blue eyes, with perfect tits. She was hot as hell, man."

"Well what happened?" I asked anxiously.

"I nailed her which was awesome but she came with some baggage. Turns out she had a boyfriend who found out and came at me after work one night. What a punk, I kicked his ass and she ended up quitting the next day. It was probably for the best though, the last thing we needed was him coming back during service and causing a scene. It wouldn't be the first time crazy shit like that has happened, it can all lead to bad buzz which is the last thing Victor wants." He said butchering some beef tenderloins.

"Victor?" I asked.

"Victor Payne, he's the guy who's invested in the place. He knows restaurants well but above all, knows the power of the press. He's a marketing genius who knows half of Manhattan. He can spin it all but he always says keep your nose clean in this town, and if you can't, don't get caught getting it dirty."

"So will I ever get to meet this Victor Payne?" I asked eagerly.

"Well, you don't work at night. He's here four or five times a week."

"I work tonight Chef, don't forget," I said smiling.

"Well if he's in here I'll introduce you," he said, finishing the tenderloin.

"Thanks Chef, that would be great."

"You got it kiddo, now let's finish up here as quickly as possible, you have a station to set up."

"Yes sir," I said respectfully.

For the next couple of hours I was heads-down in concentration. Chef moved like lightning in the kitchen. He had six sauce pots going, three sauté pans sizzling away, two ovens full of food, a half full grill and he always had something chopping on his cutting board. He was the fastest, most organized guy I'd ever seen in a kitchen. He did more in the few hours we worked together than Craig and

Fezzy combined could have done, and he never got one spot on his perfectly white coat. I did my best to keep up, but he kept having me do the chop-chop stuff that took time to do. Even though my projects were time-consuming in the end they looked great and he took notice. We finished prepping around 1:00, the time that most of the early bird cooks started to come in. The next thing I knew I was setting up an actual station in the kitchen. I was happy to be in the right place at the right time and eager to have my chance to shine. This was the Dexter House and I was a line cook, even if just for a day it was a really big deal.

I didn't speak much mainly just concentrating on what I needed to accomplish. My station was the Garde Manger, or cold food station. It wasn't just dressing salads like I'd done in the past; I had to prepare dishes like cocoa-cured duck breast with Chilean greens and ponzu vinaigrette, and Artic prawns with rice wine glaze and beet green salad. I had never worked with food like this before, but I wasn't about to let anyone know that. My father always told me, "Act like you've been in the end zone before, only rookies dance when they get there." I wasn't about to let anyone know that this was my first game in this league.

Service began and I must admit, I was a little nervous. I could see other cooks laughing and joking about things they did the night before, girls, food, but not me, I wasn't that loose. I just kind of stayed in the corner and minded my own business.

"Are you ready for a big night?" It was Chef, standing over my shoulder. He had a smile on his face that calmed me instantly.

"As ready as I can be," I replied, rubbing my sweaty hands on my apron.

"You know, I can tell you're a little nervous Jack, but you shouldn't be. That's my job," he said soothingly. I guess he'd seen the look before because I was nervous but was trying hard not to show it. I was concentrating and blocking everything else out. This is what I'd been waiting for.

"It's just, I don't want to let you down, so I'm trying to be ready for anything."

"You can't let me down kid, do you know how I know that?" he said quietly.

"No Chef, how?" I asked very curiously.

"Because of them." He signaled over his shoulder at the other cooks. They were now in full uniform, sharpening their knives, and putting the finishing touches on their stations. "They're rare. You're rare. The dedication you've shown me in these last weeks is rare. These guys have barely taken the time to get to know your name, but when the shit hits the fan tonight and you fall down, they'll be there to pick you up, dust you off, and lend you a hand. And when you fall—and fall you may—I know my guys will show you why they belong here, and why you do too. They'll make you believe in the respect both they and I have grown to command. You say you want to be a chef one day, today is your day. Even though I hold the title, if you're in this kitchen, you're already a chef."

"Thank you Chef, I won't let you down," I said proudly after hearing Chef's inspiring speech.

"I know you won't, I've got a feeling about you. Now go kick some ass." He gave me a wink and a nod of approval, turned, and left.

We were open for business. Chef Mike was in the dining room saying hello to some guests that he knew. Chef taught me that they are always guests, never customers. Customers were people who buy shoes and perfume. We spent more time at the restaurant than our own homes, which made this our home and made them our guests. People loved him, I could see them all laughing and hugging him as he spoke. He turned back into the kitchen.

"Chef on the line!" Our sous chef Lance Isaacs said militaristically as Chef Mike walked on the line. He placed his high hat on and walked the line, examining everyone's stations to ensure they were set up. If you were ready, he shook your hand and wished you luck for that night. If you were not ready, he told you what you needed and sent you to get it. Poor set-ups had consequences; Chef determined what the severity was based on how much you missed and he would inform you privately. Chef inspected my station that day as I watched nervously. "Good luck tonight," he said, shaking my hand.

Service began and the tickets came in fast, especially in the beginning for me, because my station was all appetizers. I had to open oysters to order; while I wasn't the fastest, I did my best. I plated more than 30 prawn dishes, 40 or so duck appetizers, and more than 20 light spring mix salads with fresh herbs and Champagne vinaigrette. In the first two hours of service, I did more than 100 plates. Chef watched me closely as I cleanly moved past my first rush. Just plating food was not enough; everything, especially in a restaurant of this stature, had to be plated immaculately. Most of the dishes had delicate ingredients, and our work was judged on our finesse and cleanliness. Chef stressed that it's not just about banging out food in volume—everything down to the garnish had to be pristine. Once the first wave was over, I restocked and got ready for my second push. It came almost as quickly as the first one, but harder. I thought everything was under control until I got hit hard with oysters. I had to open more than 60 as my printer was just spitting out order tickets. I fell behind, and then I got sloppy. I mis-plated a duck, and Chef noticed right away.

"You need a hand down here Jack?" one of the cooks asked.

"No . . . I . . . I only need ten more oysters opened and then I got it," I said, looking at my board full of tickets. Falling behind was the worst; it leads to what cooks commonly call "the weeds," which basically refers to being lost in a high patch of weeds unable to see the way out. You often get there due to poor mise en place, or preparation, either mental or physical. Once you're in the weeds it's tough to get out, and sometimes you just need to get plain bailed out.

"I'll help you plate those," I heard a voice say. It was the sous chef, Lance. He had left his station to come down to help me out.

"Thank you Chef Lance," I said, "I only need four spring green salads, the rest I can do."

"You got it kid." He made them in less than three minutes, and was gone. Turning around to check on the oysters, they too were already opened, plated, and waiting for me. Someone had swooped in and did them for me too. I finished up with my other dishes and was done. I looked around at my once full and ready station to find empty containers, no food, and a big mess.

"Garde Manger, all tickets in. Clean up," Lance said loudly.

"Yes Chef Lance," I replied. "Thank you."

I cleaned up fast, so as not to disturb the other cooks who still had much to accomplish. When I was done, I stood quietly in the corner watching everyone else, hoping I could return the favor.

"Garde Manger, check out with Chef and go home," Lance said again.

"Can I do anything for anyone before I go, Chef Lance?" I asked anxiously.

"No Jack, we got it from here. Good work."

"Thank you Chef." I picked up my knife and went to get changed for that long bus ride home. After all, I had much to do again the next day.

As I was walking out I heard someone clearing his throat behind me. I turned.

"You know," it was Chef Mike, "most people celebrate after victories like that one."

"I wouldn't exactly call that a victory, it took two people to bail me out," I said glumly.

"When Lance first started, it took four. And one of them had to stay on that station all night. Only one person since we opened had a first night like that," he said seriously.

"Who was that, Chef?" I asked.

"That was me. And if we weren't just opening, I might have needed more. Congratulations Jack, that was better than anyone could have hoped for. How about joining me for a glass of wine?" he asked proudly.

"It would be an honor," I responded.

CHAPTER 7

MEET VICTOR PAYNE

Chef and I sat in the upstairs VIP loft and he ordered a bottle of Far Niente 1992, a California wine that was about $400 a bottle. "You got it Chef," the bartender said as Mike turned and headed to his table. He had washed up and was wearing a pair of jeans and a purple button down shirt without a wrinkle on it.

Every one of the 50 seats in the room was taken. The room was dark, and the views were amazing: the New York skyline on one side, and a glass wall that overlooked The Dexter House dining room on the other. No surprise, Mike's booth overlooked the restaurant. The booths by the window made you feel like you reeked of power; the diners looked so small and they constantly looked up to the VIP loft. Loud pop music blasted through the speakers as the who's who of New York enjoyed the exclusivity of the room. Not everyone was welcomed into the upstairs loft of the Dexter House—it was reserved for the most elite New York had to offer. The room had been graced by New York's mayor, Rudy Giuliani; actors like Tom Hanks and Jerry Seinfeld; New Yorkers like Spike Lee and Billy Crystal; and the city's most respected, highfalutin' doctors and high-powered attorneys and politicians made their way up there. It was members only, and God only knows what it took to become a member. We sat on our plush tufted bench and put our elbows on the thick oak table that held a single candle and a drink menu. Chef put his hands behind his head and looked over the crowd. He was the real star here.

"Do you know what someone is who never grows or changes Jack?" Chef asked me in a serious voice.

"No Chef?" I responded, confused.

"They're a building, they never change. At first they're shinny and new, but after a while, they get old. They were designed, thought out, built, and then decorated all by other people, and from other people's visions. They never quite have their own identities. After a while they get old. People don't care for them the way they used to. In time they can ruin entire neighborhoods around them, until someone comes with a new vision, and knocks them down." He took a sip of wine.

"Chef?" I said again, more confused now.

"But then," he turned around quickly, "there's trees. Trees grow on their own, nobody had to design them, they're all natural, organic. If you look right at them, they don't seem to change much either, but they do. They grow. They stand tall through all the hard times, all the bad weather, and when the sun shines on them, they bloom. Take a picture of one some time, and look at it again in ten years, you'll see how much that tree has slowly grown." He stood up and handed me a glass of wine. "New York has a lot of buildings in it Jack, but trees are rare." He raised his glass for a toast.

I paused, thinking of what he had said. "Don't think that you're built after one day, the naturals keep slowly growing kid." He took a sip from his wine, wiped his mouth and then started laughing. "You kicked ass tonight, man," he shouted, putting his arm around me."

It was then that I heard a new voice behind me; it was a moment I would never forget. It was a deep, chalky-sounding voice, which had a sound of confidence pouring out of it of which the likes I had never heard. "Look at 'em, just look at all of 'em, all the self-proclaimed beautiful people in this easy come, easy go paradise we call NEW YORK, here at this place for one person only!"

"Well, you do draw a good crowd," Chef said to him, chuckling.

"For you Michael, they're all here for you," he said, walking closer. A thin man, 5'8, about 50 years old with black hair parted down the middle and a healthy looking face smiled as he approached Mike. He wore a tuxedo with his bow tie undone, and traveled with a couple of really attractive women. He was smoking a cigar and carrying a bottle of 1940 Del Poile au Vin, which sold for about $2000 a bottle in one hand and two glasses in the other. A waiter came racing to him with a table, a wine bucket, and table setting. They pulled up chairs for the women.

"Will you be needing anything for the moment Mr. Payne?" the waiter asked. The man gave him $50 and replied, "Not for the moment Jimmy, but don't go far."

"Yes sir Mr. Payne." He raced away as quick as he came.

"Another successful night I see Chef," he said, extending his hand towards Chef as he took a seat.

"It was modest, not as full as it could have been," Chef replied.

"You say that so glumly for a man whose sales are up more than 50% for the quarter, ha!" He gave him a big pat on the back. "Please, join me for a drink, it's been a long night, political bullshit event after political bullshit event."

"You're a tough man to say no to Vic," Chef said smiling.

"No, I'm easy. It's all the great wine I have that's tough to say no to, eh Michael," he said, slapping him on the back.

"I guess it's a little of both." The two of them had a good laugh.

"Vic, this is Jack Cahill, our intern from the CIA; he did the work of four people today, literally. Jack, meet Victor Payne," Chef said proudly.

"Ah, CIA huh, you're exactly the type of worker we like to have here at The Dexter House," he said, shaking my hand.

"And what kind of worker is that?" I asked curiously.

"The free kind, ha!" He started laughing out loud and raising his eyebrows. He had definitely been drinking, but in a good way. Laughing, he said, "I'm just kidding with you young man, please, take a seat, it's nice to meet you. So Mike, what's been going on here lately?" he asked, sitting down. It was strange listening to people call him Mike, and not Chef.

"Business as usual," he said calmly.

"You know, that's why I love this guy, give him an opportunity to sit here and gripe with the boss and he never wants to talk business. That, and he's the best damn chef New York has ever seen."

"He sure is, and the best looking," one of the ladies said from across the table.

"Hey, hey quiet down over there now," Victor said playfully. "In fact, my chef and I do need to discuss some business so why don't you girls hit the bar and order us up some more of this wine, but see if they have it in a 1938, it was a much better year," he said to the ladies. "What about you Jack, want a glass?" he asked me.

"I'd love one, thanks," I said nervously. The girls got up and left. Victor leaned in and I stayed and tried hard to act like my attention was averted.

"So Mike, I just wanted to say thanks for last week's reception. Governor Pataki called and said he had never seen such a beautifully plated, well-executed party. How you made that foie gras and sea urchin terrine for 700 people was beyond me. Did you see the cover of the *Times* the next day?"

"Yeah, it was a great picture of you Vic," Chef said.

"No . . . I mean yes it was, and thank you by the way, but I was talking about the paragraph where they talked about you and the food?"

"Yes, I did," Chef replied.

"And do you know why I'm telling you this?" Victor said.

"Because never in history has a catered political reception made mention of the company that catered it," Chef responded, sipping his wine.

"Goddamn Mike, nothing gets past you. HA! You are even sharper than I give you credit for. Not only did you get mentioned, but they wrote more than 200 words about us. We are hot! We need to strike now; this is just one piece of press in the file cabinet full of press that you've been getting lately. You're everywhere Mike, like nothing this town has ever seen! So, Chef, what do you propose?" he asked. I was just sitting comfortably, wondering if I should stay or go.

"Well Victor, you know as well as I do that press only lasts so long, eventually they'll write about something or someone else unless we keep their eyes on us. Dexter's maxed out, we're at capacity so we only have one option—another unit—but why stop there? We have a lot of talent under this roof, enough for four more units, larger-than-life units, to take this town by storm. We can do that, I can do that for us."

Victor laughed and looked stunned. "Why four Michael?"

"Because with four more restaurants, each matching or exceeding our current revenue here, we would be the highest grossing independently owned operation in Manhattan. Only the corporations would have more, and even those are few. With the press and the *New York Times* on our side, to the point where I got in more quotes at last week's Ball then Hillary Clinton did, I know we could do that, we have what it takes but we all know no one sits on top forever, no one. Eventually even the greatest kings get dethroned, so we build to sell. Our goal will be build them, establish them, push 'em to the max and sell them as a unit. There's so much goddamn money in this town and in this restaurant alone, to sell would be easy. To sell would be profit on an enormous scale. Now," he paused and leaned in towards Victor, "aren't you even going to offer me a cigar Vic?" Chef said coolly.

"They're Cubans," Victor said, astonished.

"I know." Chef took the cigar from Victor and lit it up. "I was counting on it."

"HA! You clever son of a bitch! You sly bastard! You never cease to amaze me Mike. Hot damn I want to be like Mike too!" Victor turned to me and said, "It's not all just chopping onions now, is it kid? HA! This guy is proof of that!"

"I'd hoped it wasn't," I responded, just happy to be there at all.

Victor grabbed Mike's face, squeezing his cheeks. "This guy is a testament to your industry, kid. It's called the restaurant 'business' for a reason!" he said, letting go of Mike but still laughing jovially. "Pay attention, you've got to have one hell of a head on your shoulders to make it big in this business. Talent too, of course, but to make it to the top you've got to know every detail. Mikey, you are my most trusted confidant, as always you know exactly what I'm thinking!" he said in a loud, halting manner. "Well Mike, that's it, if everything goes right I'll retire a very wealthy man soon. And there's only one person I trust to make sure everything goes smoothly. I think you know who that is. How does 8% sound, Mike?"

"It sounds better than five but not as good as ten," he said smiling.

"You blue collared bandit, ha, I knew you were gonna say that. All right don't twist any tighter; if you want it, you've got yourself a deal, partner. Let's celebrate! I love this guy!" he said, giving Chef a big hug.

That was the way Victor made deals. In less than two minutes, he gave Chef an opportunity of a lifetime. Victor was more like a celebrity than a restaurateur. He knew Chef was the only one for the job, and Victor could make $250 million in less than two years if everything went right and Mike stood to make 10% of that. One thing Victor knew was that you had to strike while you're hot, and he had the money, the mind, and the manpower to accomplish anything. He also knew how to have a good time.

Once business was concluded Victor was all good times, and man what a party he could throw. He was flamboyantly generous with everything, walking around pouring wine for anyone with a glass in hand. The whole upstairs was dancing and drinking thousands of dollars in wine. We smoked cigars and sang all night. There were women all over Victor, and Chef disappeared for a while with a woman who was in town from LA to model for a Guess Jeans ad. These guys were bigger than life. With the names they had, they could do no wrong. I had the privilege of speaking with Victor for a while; he put his arm around me and gave me his view on the business. In a world where they say 90% of all restaurants fail in the first year, and the best way to make a million dollars in the restaurant business is to invest two, he said there's only one way to make it. It's a business full of moving pieces, often dictated by the variety of personalities that touch the business every day, both employees and guests. He said most people don't stand a chance because they never learn how to control it, concluding, "In order to control the chaos, you have to become the chaos." Those words never left my head and though I was new and lacked their experience, I knew exactly what he meant. We didn't talk shop for long. We drank some amazing wine and vodka together; he was incorrigible but in the best way possible, and he made the night unforgettable for everyone there.

Around 4am things were winding down. Victor was drunk, but still able to sing "New York, New York" at the top of his lungs. Chef was doing well; he nestled up at the bar with the Guess model and was sipping a tequila drink. Looking at him closely I could see fatigue settling in. I was beyond excited to be there, but it was time for me to go. I went up to Chef and said, "I think I may call it a night Chef." I had overstayed my welcome anyway.

"That's probably not such a bad idea, I'll probably be right behind you." He stood up to shake my hand. "Thanks again for tonight Jack, it's guys like you that make guys like me look good." We shook hands and I turned to go.

As I walked away I turned back and Chef was still looking at me. I waved goodbye, and he called out, "Jack!" I turned and saw him approaching me. "Even if they get cut down, the tough ones grow back stronger than ever." I nodded gratefully and headed home.

CHAPTER 8

MISSED OPPORTUNITIES

My days in Manhattan were limited at that point. I couldn't believe that night of celebration, I mean the glamour and the glitz was too much, it was something I never wanted to leave. Victor was intoxicating, his lifestyle was unparalleled but he was miles ahead of where I was and I needed to keep that in mind. Mike always said this business is about a slow rise, earning your keep and advancing at a specific pace. It's a long journey, one that no matter how hard you try, you can't force. The ones who force it become frustrated, an emotion that has no place in this business. Patience, you need lots and lots of patience.

I was into my final week and it was so ordinary. Chef was always cool, but I was back to finishing out the rest of my externship. We didn't hang out again; in fact, I hardly saw him, and I was getting so fast that I was gone early every day. It didn't matter though. Eggplant caviar, 50 pounds of onions, chopping parsley, it just seemed so remedial. I felt like I'd graduated past that. Nonetheless, I was still the low man, I was still working for free, my aspirations had to be muted, I still had school in front of me and still had time to bide.

On my last day before heading back upstate to the CIA, Chef had to fill out my externship evaluation book. I had to write a 20-page logbook and get it graded on my performance. Chef and I sat down at the end of my shift to review it so he could grade me.

"So, this is it, huh Jack?" he said, sitting down with me in the dining room. He had a cup of coffee and gave me a look of assurance before he graded me. I handed him my log book. "I don't even need to open this one," he said, putting it down on the table, he signed the cover and put down an "A" where it said grade. "You know you play everything pretty cool Jack, that's unusual for a 18- year-old kid. You also exceeded our expectations here." He said handing me my logbook back.

"Thank you Chef, that means a lot coming from you," I responded proudly.

"You know, most cooks have a tendency to misconstrue things. Did you have a good time hanging out with us the other night?" he asked nudging his head upward towards the

VIP loft. It was always funny being in the dining room by day; we used the tables for desks, and power seats for coffee breaks. He asked as if that question even needed an answer.

"Of course, it was the most fun I think I've ever had," I replied. "But I'm just happy for you. Is Victor serious about the restaurant openings?" I asked.

"Victor is always serious about his business," Chef replied. "And it didn't seem to impress you. Hearing you say that it was the most fun you ever had comes as news to me. You didn't show it; in fact, you don't ever seem to show any emotion when you're on the job. You're focused and you have purpose. Even Victor noticed."

"Did he say anything to you about me?" I asked eagerly.

"No," Chef replied slowly, "but he will today when he comes to talk to you." He smiled, picking my book up off the table.

"Victor is coming here?" I asked stunned. "What for?"

"Go ahead and ask him yourself," Chef said, looking up. There was Victor, right on cue as usual.

"Ask me what, Mr. Cahill?" he said, patting Chef on the shoulder and looking me straight in the eye.

"I was just telling Jack that you were coming to see him and he was inquiring as to why," Chef replied casually He stood up and pulled out his chair, "Would you like to sit and talk Mr. Payne?" he asked again very shadily.

"I would Chef, and thank you. Could you have Lance put a steak on the grill for me? I haven't eaten since breakfast," Victor responded, looking me right in the eye.

"What kind?" Chef asked.

Victor looked up at him as he sat, tucking his napkin into his shirt and said, "Surprise me."

Chef nodded and walked away. Victor looked at me, again directly in the eye and said, "Missed opportunity. That's what kills people in life. Can you think of the last opportunity you missed Jack?"

"No sir?" I responded curiously.

"Well, you have missed two since I've sat down already." A waiter came up and poured him some water and left. "Three," he said, staring at me.

"Sir I'm confused," I said.

"Well, you had a chance to eat something when I ordered, and you missed an opportunity to impress me by remembering the last missed one you had." He took a sip of water. "Ah!" he said refreshed, then he said slowly, "and you didn't ask the waiter for any water. Tell me why?" he asked, taking another sip.

"I didn't think it was my place," I said with a little stutter, which was rare for me. Victor could make anyone feel on edge; he was unpredictable and impulsive, and he liked to try to catch people off guard. His steak was quickly delivered and he immediately started to eat.

He took a bite and smiled, still chewing. "Well, if you're hungry then it's your place, if you're thirsty it's your place, but if you're feeling out of place then it never will be," he said, leaning in towards me. "Missed opportunities my boy, that leads to regret, regret leads to frustration, frustration blinds talent. Desire Jack, desire to reach out and take life by its cojones! That's what drives this business, it fuels you, keeps you on edge, where you need to be," he said, taking another sip. As he did, his server Kaitlin came over and asked, "Mr. Payne, do you need anything?" She was adorable, with short red hair and a small scrunched face with freckles and glasses. She had a killer body, and her uniform hugged her like a glove.

I leaned back, just a little, almost to act uninterested. I didn't want to miss another opportunity for Victor's sake so I said, "It's my last day and I'm a little hungry. I never spoke to you before, and I was wondering if you wouldn't mind getting something to eat with me?"

"What, now? Here? How?" she asked, confused. She shot a look in Victor's direction.

"Victor, you don't mind if we sit and get some food a little before opening today, do you?" I said.

"No, that would be fine Jack," Victor replied with his mouth full. He swallowed and said, "The only problem is I need to meet with you. I'm sure the beautiful young lady will be happy to take a rain check," he said, reaching for his newly added glass of wine.

"Is a rain check OK?"

"I guess it has to be." She took out a piece of paper and wrote down her phone number. "Here. For you, this being your last day and all. Call me some time Jack, I'd love to hang out," she said, handing me her number. She turned and got back to work and I turned my attention back to Victor.

Victor said, "I was scouting Michael since he was 18 years old. He used to work in a bar down in the village called Duet. He was a scrappy cook. He had that orange beard, that big bright orange beard." He laughed as he described it. "Mike was good at what he did. I spent a lot of time in his bar—this was long before all the glory of the Dexter house, of course. I was looking to open up my own place. I already had money from investing in another restaurant in Brooklyn called Celsius. It was a little raw bar and fish house. We only had 50 seats or so, but we filled them to capacity every night. When I sold my portion out, I took the same concept to midtown and named the place The Big Raw Bar. It was a great concept, but I needed somebody to run it. I called on Mike. I paid him a fair wage, and he worked for every last cent that he got. This kid was as good as gold. He worked his fingers to the bone. He and I brought the Big Raw Bar to massive status. We filled it to the point where I thought the walls would explode, I mean full, full, full, every single night from open to close. When I sold it to buy the Dexter House, I invested everything I had in Michael's vision. I love restaurants, and everything about the business, but I don't know anything about running them, at least not like he does. That's were Mike comes in, and that's where you'll come in."

Another waiter came to top off Victor's water. As he did Victor ordered some wine, "I'll have some of that as well," I said.

Victor nodded at me. "You learn fast son," he said, extending his glass for a toast. We clinked glasses. "You know, I've shaken hands with every big shot chef there is in this city. I took Mike and I didn't look back. He likes you. I like you. We have good eyes for rare talent, but I don't want you today." He paused to drink.

"Well when do you want me?" I asked, drinking my wine.

"You got the girl. She wants you, that was impressive and impulsive. Do you know why she wants you? Because of who you know. That 'who you know' attitude is in your system, you want to harness it, but you can't yet, you don't know how. You're like an unripe peach. When you ripen, you'll know, and that's when I'll be there. You're a one in seven chance to me. Work on upping the ratio before we meet again," he said, finishing his wine. "Chef, come over here."

Chef came out from around the corner. "How is everything?"

"I know you made this for me," he said, pointing at his empty plate.

"Well, Lance was a little tired."

"You're the only knife in the city, Mike, that never gets dull," he said, extending his hand.

"Thank you sir." Chef shook his hand and gave him a half hug.

"You keep an eye on this one Mike, we need more like him. Good luck kid. Chef Jack Cahill, we'll see you soon. Thanks, Chef, for another fabulous meal." He patted Chef on the chest, gave me a wink, and left.

I stood up, "So Chef, I guess this is good-bye." I extended my hand.

"No it isn't, it's more like see you later." Chef shook my hand and smiled, as he looked me in the eye. "I'll see you soon."

"Yeah, see you soon." I picked up my stuff and turned to leave. Chef was already heading back to the kitchen.

"Hey Chef," I yelled. He stopped, but didn't turn around. "Thank you," I said meaningfully. Chef put his arm in the air, threw a slow motion fist pump, and started walking again. I hoped he was right; that we would see each other soon, but for now it was back upstate for me. As I walked out I felt like I was closing a major chapter in my life. I had grown so much in the last months. I didn't want to leave, but all good things come to an end at some point, and it was time to get back to Hyde Park. There was still much to be done there.

CHAPTER 9

REMEMBER ME?

I returned to the CIA with a whole new outlook. I hadn't spoken to any of my classmates while I was on my externship and I doubt they even thought about me. I hardly thought about them, except for Karen. Sometimes when I was in the city, I would see her face. I knew that sleeping with Molly had probably ruined any chance I had with her so I tried to block her out, but there she was, in my head. Some nights no matter how hard I tried I couldn't get her out.

I was in evening classes now, so they didn't start until 1pm. My first class back was Baking and Pastry 101. I arrived about twenty minutes early just to get reacquainted with my classmates. When I walked in, Tom and Molly were talking with Brad and a couple of other people. I didn't see Karen, but I went over to say hello.

"Oh my God!" Molly screamed, running towards me as soon as she saw me. She grabbed me and gave me a huge hug, "What the hell!" she yelled, "Where have you been? It's like you fell off the map!"

"New York," I replied, hugging her back and smiling.

"Hey Jack, how was the Big Apple?" Tom said, patting me on the back as Molly was still holding me.

"Short but sweet big guy, how was your externship? I missed you guys," I said, embracing them.

"Great, I learned a lot about this shit," Tom said sarcastically while giving a half smile and laughing. "Well, nonetheless, it's good to be in the home stretch."

"I agree," interjected Molly.

Just then Karen walked in. She was dressed in her culinary whites with her hair down, and smiling from ear to ear. She stopped to say hello to some friends and as she was hugging one of them, our eyes met. I nodded shyly as she glanced at me.

I continued making chit-chat with Tom and Molly but I could hardly hear one word they were saying. My ears were ringing with Karen's presence; it was like she was floating throughout the room. I watched coolly as she spoke to her friends and exchanged secret glances with me. Looking at her was like something out of a dream.

After a couple of minutes of aimless nodding and quick one-liners to Tom and Molly, I was anxious to speak with

Karen. No matter what I'd done or seen in New York, she was still the biggest thing to me. I just hope she'd forgotten about Molly and I. Even though she was with Tommy, I still didn't want her to think about it.

She hugged the people she was talking to and moved on to us. She went straight for Molly and gave her a huge hug. They screamed and hugged for about a minute and then she turned to me.

"Hey Karen, how was your externship?" I asked her nervously, as she turned to give me a kiss on the cheek and a big embrace.

"Great!" she said, "I learned so much." She let go of me and turned to Tom who gave her a hug and a long kiss on the cheek.

"I missed you baby," he said, picking her up off her feet and smiling. Maybe those two had something that nobody saw; maybe they were actually happy together.

"I missed you too Tom," she said, patting him on the chest and leaning away from his kisses. He gruffly tried to keep her close.

"What's wrong baby," he said, noticeably insulted, and as usual quite pissed-off.

"Nothing," she said as he placed her back on the ground, "we're just in class, that's all." The two of them stopped hugging.

"OK, it's cool babe, we'll catch up after class," Tom said. He was acting like they were together, and maybe they were; I had been totally out of touch.

"Sure, sounds great," she said, pulling her hair back behind her ears and looking to the ground. Just then the chef walked in. In the CIA, we had very few actual professors—they were mostly chef instructors who were, in many cases, the best in their fields. Our instructor was Chef Panini, a world-renowned pastry chef.

"Welcome back students, is everyone ready to take on the world now?" he asked in a playfully sarcastic manner. Chef Panini was a short Italian man with a thick accent and a prominent brown mustache. Everyone laughed at his statement and started to pay attention. "Now, please be seated." He said smiling. As he did we all sat and I noticed Karen give Molly a look, and then she glanced towards me and half smiled. I hadn't laid eyes on her for months, but I did think about her every night and I was actually happy to be back because she was here.

"Welcome to the exciting world of bread baking!" Chef Panini began his lecture. Although the course was informative, I had a hard time paying attention. Class went more quickly than I thought. We did a few practicals, made some bread, and took a quick day one test at the end. At the CIA there was no grace period; they put you right into production. You either know it or you don't on day one, and if you don't by day two, you fail. So to make sure you go on with your team you have to be well prepared for each block. This class was particularly challenging because not only was it technical, it was our first one back so it was a healthy dose of reality that we weren't on externship anymore but back on campus, and we had to pay attention in totally different ways.

At the end of class everyone flocked out to the main courtyard to catch up and talk about their externships. The brick laid courtyard was right in the center of all the buildings on campus. It had a large quaint fountain, the signature CIA clock, and was surrounded by well-groomed landscaping. It was a nice place to relax either before or after class, and most students did. There was a popular cappuccino kiosk that always had a few people in line, even though the coffee sucked. At night it was well lit with white Christmas lights year round, and dim spotlights overhead. It was a great place to unwind. I found Brad and our friend John and started to reminisce a little.

"Hey Cahill, so you coming to my party tonight?" he asked, elbowing me in the arm.

"I thought you only had parties on the weekends," I said, happy to be talking with these guys again.

"We're in night classes now baby! We can party all the time," he said, laughing it up as good-natured as he always was.

"Yeah man, I'll be there."

"Come on by anytime Cahill, we'll be going all night," Brad said, slapping my hand.

"See you in a bit, man," I said, turning away. I looked around the courtyard, but Karen had already left. I guess she wasn't as anxious to talk to me as I was to talk to her.

I made small talk with a few other people, just catching up briefly as I walked out of the courtyard heading to my car, but I didn't get that involved. As I approached my car, I don't think a more pleasant surprise could have appeared.

"Well well well, if it isn't Mr. New York himself. You know, if you weren't always trying to play mayor, you would have been here a lot sooner." It was Karen, leaning on my driver's side door, smiling as always.

"How was Delaware?" I asked, stopping in my tracks and starting to fidget with my car keys.

"Really nice, it was good to be back home for a while; it gave me a lot of time to think."

"Well, thinking is a good thing right?" I asked.

"It can be. Depends what you're thinking about, I guess," she said, tilting her head and taking a breath.

"What was it that kept your mind moving so much?" I asked, taking one step closer.

"A lot of things, I guess."

"Name one," I said, taking another step.

"Well. . . . It . . . It was too many to . . ." She squirmed a little and folded her arms. She put her head down. I took one more step in and touched her lightly on the chin; she looked up at me nervously. I was in a state of complete calm. "Just name one, Karen," I said, soothingly.

"That look you give me, for one," she said, pulling away and standing up straight. "And the way I feel when you do." She started to walk away quickly. I tried to grab her arm but she started to pull away.

"What is so wrong with that!" I yelled as she ran away.

"A lot is, Jack, do you want me to get started?" she said, turning around but still heading away.

"Do you want to tell me what the hell that is?!" I asked back. She stopped and looked over her shoulder. "Why do you always hold back from me?"

"Are you serious, after what I did to you that night, I had the hardest time even talking to you before we left," she said, taking a step back. "You were the same way to me, you never tried for me again after that night, and you just went through the rest of the semester looking at me awkwardly. I never blamed you though, after I left you that night, I had a hard time even facing you. You said the sweetest things to me, things that still echo in my heart today. I would try to explain what happened, but I'm sure it's pointless to even try."

"Karen, all I've done for the last few months was think about the things I did to screw things up as well." I began walking over to her. "You have nothing to explain to me, I've been waiting for this moment ever since you closed the door that night. All I've wanted since then was to be here, right here, with those eyes of yours, looking at me. Every time I see them, it's like the first time all over again."

She walked quickly over to me and gave me a big hug. "We were so close that night Jack, I would give anything to go back and do it all over again," she said, pulling back with her arms still around me. "And what did you do to screw things up Jack, I was the one, what could you possibly have to be sorry about?"

"You know that night, after you left," I said slowly.

"Yeah? What about it?" she asked, dumbfounded.

"Well, I drank that bottle of wine alone, I waited for you, I waited for hours and ended up getting pretty drunk sitting there. I wasn't myself, you know."

"I know Jack, that must have sucked. I feel like shit over the whole thing really. When I got back to my room and you had gone home, I just felt terrible. Then I felt worse when I saw the empty wine bottle. The first thing I wanted to do was call you, you had that drive and it was late, I was just worried. When I saw you the next day, I was just relieved. I don't blame you for shying away from me until now. I know I felt a little weird after that. That's why I was so strange there for a while, I just thought you wouldn't believe me if I told you."

"Try me," I said, leaning in.

"Buy me a drink first?" she said smiling at me.

"Brad's having people over, you want to swing by there?" I asked.

"No," she said looking up at me. "Tonight I just want to be with you."

As we walked across the street to the bar, I was facing the realization that Karen had absolutely no idea that I'd slept with Molly that night. I was in disbelief that Molly had never told her. That whole time before our externships she was just acting that way because she felt guilty. I could have said something to make things work. We went inside and sat down at the bar. I ordered us a couple of beers and we started talking. I pulled out a smoke and lit it up.

"Those things will kill you," Karen said to me.

"I've heard that once or twice before," I replied, leaning back. "So, I'm ready, tell me about it."

"First of all," she said, taking a swig of beer, "it's not what you think. What I'm going to tell you will not be easy for you to hear."

I interrupted, "Look, you guys are like boyfriend, girlfriend, it's not my place to say—"

"He was going to kill himself," she said, silencing the mood. I just sat there. She looked at me for a second or two and then said, "He was going to kill himself because I told him I was in love with someone else."

I sat silent for a second, collecting my thoughts. I had never dealt with the reality of suicide. I was deeply concerned about my friend, but selfishly and almost uncontrollably, in this moment I wanted it to be about us. I leaned in and asked, looking her straight in the eye, "In . . . love . . . with?"

She grabbed my hand, "Yes," she said, touching my face, "in love with." She leaned in and gave me a soft kiss on my forehead, then my lips. "You're the first person I've ever met who I believe in my heart would never hurt me. I believe in that, I think you're so caring and thoughtful, and have always treated me with the utmost respect. I think you're great Jack Cahill, and I don't care who knows."

I was stunned. This was a lot at one time. "And what about Tom, how is he about this?" I asked, concerned.

"He's gotten better. I mean, that night I spoke to him for hours, he showed me the note for God's sake, it was chilling. I needed to be there to talk him out of it. He knew we were over, or rather, never really started, it was just a lot. He almost had to drop out because he couldn't afford to go to school anymore."

"Can't he take out a loan or something?"

"Well, he has one now, but at the time he was on his own and his loans never came through. Tom is very different behind the scenes, he's scared of life."

"And how is he now?"

"Now, I don't know, I'm not behind stage anymore. That part of my life is over. I have too many problems with my own life and I don't have time for his too, at least not any longer."

"Today you seemed like you'd stayed in touch over your externs, he was grabby and flirty, was I seeing things?" I said as I put out my smoke in the oversized ashtray.

"That's just him, he's been weird. Ever since that night I've tried to play along with his oddities but not lead him on. He knows we're over, but he still has these bizarre tendencies," she said, grabbing her beer and pulling down a big sip. "As much as I feel bad we only went out briefly, I mean very briefly, and enough time has gone by that he needs to finally understand that I just can't make his problems mine, no matter how serious they are. I know that makes me sound like a totally mean person but I'm not, he's a grown man and he's not my problem. I feel awful but I just don't have the time, especially because we are not now and haven't been together for such a long period."

"Do you have time for mine?" I asked Karen. Her eyes just melted me.

She finished her beer and stood up, grabbing my hand, "I'll make time, let's go."

We left Shenanigans quickly. She was practically running out the door. We raced back to her dorm and shut the door behind us. "So," Karen said with her back to me, "let's try this again." She turned around holding the exact bottle of wine as last time. She turned on some music, poured us each a glass, and toasted to another try. "Do you want to smoke a joint?" she asked me, laughing.

"Yeah, why not?" I said.

We sat there all night talking, drinking wine, smoking, and laughing, just curled up on some pillows by the window. I think it may have been the single greatest, and most simple night of my whole life. No glamour, no glitz, no nothing, just her and me with nothing but time. I was in love with her. Around 2am I turned out the lights, she kissed me, I kissed her back and we made love like I had never done before. It was wild, exciting, heart-pounding and highly anticipated. It lasted all night and was pure passion. I had been with other women and she had been with other men but nothing felt like this, love made it so much more. I was totally and completely head over heels in love with her.

CHAPTER 10

WE'RE COOL

Karen and I were finally and officially together. Being with her was like walking on air. She made me a better person and a smarter chef. I worked harder when I was with her, I studied longer, I cooked faster, I rose to the top of my class, handling everything in front of me. I was strong because of her, and getting stronger by the day, and professors and chefs alike took notice.

Weeks went by faster than days and classes were so brief, some of them were as short as seven days. Most of the time we were thrust immediately into action, no warm-up, and very little getting to know you with the professors, but I think that most of the chefs talked amongst themselves behind the scenes and knew who to keep their eyes on. The school had favorites, students who were paid just a little more attention whether they admitted it or not. They knew where the talent was and they challenged it more—at least the better chefs did.

Our class had a few standouts, some you really felt were going to make a difference in the industry— the ones who followed technique, worked clean, and had the temperament to adapt and adjust. Tom was struggling, like his attention was elsewhere. He said he was over Karen, and to some degree I believed him but I wasn't sure that was it, at least not exclusively. He was drinking more; he would go MIA for whole nights at a time and show up late to class the following day. He and I would grab beers, shoot pool, throw darts, or even just cool out after class, especially on nights when Karen was studying.

One late night at Shenanigans, Tom and I were playing pool. Even when he was wasted he could shoot the shit out of the table. "It's all coming pretty easy to you these days, Jack," he said, hunched over and nailing a shot from across the table.

"I wouldn't go that far," I said, sipping my Heineken. "I do feel pretty comfortable though, how about you? You got any prospects for career day tomorrow?" The air was full of smoke and Dave Matthews Band was on the juke.

"Fuck that," he said, nailing another shot and not ever looking up from the table long enough to do anything but slug his beer. "Who goes to career day, that shit is for tools, no offense of course. Besides, what's the point, who wants to work in those corporate shitholes anyway?" He was really buzzed up.

"They're not all corporate," I said, lighting up a smoke. "There's a lot of independents there; I have my eye on a few good spots, some corporate some not. I figured it's at least worth shaking some hands and seeing what's out there."

"What, no New York after graduation?" he said, now nailing the eight ball and ending the game. He was on fire, I hadn't shot in about three games. "Rack 'em bitch," he said to me with a smile. I put down my cigarette and picked up the rack. "Losers buy shots too!" he said with a laugh.

I smiled back and said, "You know it." I waved to Brittney the bartender and said "Two Jacks when you can, Brit!" She gave me the thumbs up and brought them right over to us.

"This one's on me, and Tommy, love the way you handle your stick, maybe later we can see if I can handle it just as well," she said softly in his ear and she grazed his hips with her hand as she headed back. She was always into him. She was sexy but totally Goth and tatted up, exactly his type.

"Count on it, woman," he replied and grabbed her ass as she left. She let out a little scream and a smile as she crow-hopped away.

"To bitches like that!" he said, sticking out his glass to cheers. I stuck mine out and nodded, banging back my shot.

"Wow!" he screamed as he threw his shot back. "So where was I, oh yeah, New York, you're not heading back?" he said, chalking up his cue.

"I'm not saying I'm not, but I want to at least see what's out there, keep my options open. I guess it all depends on . . ." I hesitated before I finished my statement and it was noticeable.

"Depend on what?" he asked unsuspectingly. He was a good friend.

"I guess it depends on Karen and what she's doing," I said, picking up my smoke and taking a big drag before squishing it out.

He hesitated and took another gulp, finishing the bottle. "Jack, I want to tell you something as a friend, one of my only ones," he said, sparking up a smoke of his own. "You and Karen, I'm cool with that."

"Tom, I—" I tried interrupting like I often did, but he wasn't having it.

"Let me finish, this will only take a second. Karen and I were never going to live happily ever after, were just too different. Sure, some shit went down while we dated but normal shit, everyone does fucked up things, all relationships are fucked up, some people just hide it better. You and me are cool Jack, Karen's a great girl, a special girl." He hesitated for a second himself, almost like his mind went somewhere else for a second. "I'm glad she's with someone like you who will treat her right, the way she deserves to be treated, the way I never could." His eyes drifted away from mine which was rare, because he always looked people straight in the eye.

I had never seen that side of him before. I was honestly choked up. I had a serious look on my face, like someone just hit the reset button inside of me. It was a huge load off, one that offered me great relief. "Thanks man, that truly means a lot."

"Now stop acting like such a pussy and go get us two more beers so I can kick your ass again!' That was the Tom I knew.

CHAPTER 11

CAREER DAY

Career day at the CIA is a very big deal. It's a two-day annual event that attracts the largest and best restaurants and hotels. They gather in the Conrad Hilton Library to recruit promising young help for their establishments. The displays are grand and proud, and potential employers range from Carnival Cruise Lines, to Marriot Hotels, to corporate chains, to slick independent restaurants. Proprietors and representatives from these places take it very seriously, dressed for success and well-organized. Most require an appointment, but some accept walk-ups. The whole library is packed, corner to corner, and what a backdrop the Hilton is. From the outside it is understated, but inside it's so grand with two levels of thick wooden bookcases lined with every culinary and cookbook ever published. In the pre-Internet era it was quite an important resource. The high ceilings, arched windows, and hand painted art work on the walls offer a great place to escape and unwind, and students always did; it was usually pretty hard to get a seat at a table there because it was always bustling and full.

On that day I was interested in three particular restaurants: one in Orlando, one in San Diego, and the other in Boston. Karen had some interest in looking at jobs back in Delaware, but mostly she was focused on Boston too and was trying aggressively for a concierge position at the Four Seasons. She always talked about broadening her horizons outside of the kitchen.

Most of the interviews were brief meet-and-greets on the first day; those who make an impression get a callback for a more in-depth second interview. I interviewed with Tishio first, a steak and sushi restaurant in Mission Bay, San Diego that was recruiting three line cooks. Most places like Tishio were there with specific roles to fill. More than 100 students interviewed for the positions. I thought I spoke well and was appropriately dressed, wearing a black suit and red tie. Next I interviewed with The Moon Room, an exciting new spot in downtown Boston. They were interviewing for a sous chef position; I figured I would try even though I hadn't had that much experience. My third interview was with Walt Disney World Resorts in Orlando

Florida, for the position of lead line cook at Sing's Diner, one of the many restaurants in the resort.

After a long day of interviews Karen and I grabbed a quick dinner, then I headed home with high hopes and low expectations.

"Where's my big chef?" my mother said as I walked in the door.

"Hey Mom, how are you?" I asked, grabbing a glass of water.

"I'm great, except for the fact that your little brother can't seem to stay out of trouble," she said.

"What did he do this time?" I asked.

"I got another phone call today from the principal. Your little brother got caught raiding the girls locker room after gym class." She said looking down her glasses at me.

"I wonder where he got an idea like that?" I asked sarcastically.

"He has an older brother who was too smart for his own good, and should have put his mind on the books instead of playing pranks and chasing girls around all those years," she said, stirring the pasta sauce she was making.

"He turned out OK," I said.

"Yeah, we'll see about that, mister. Hey, speaking of phone calls, you got a couple today."

I took a sip of water. "Anyone outside the norm?" I asked.

"Well if Chef Bleu Luimar, Chef William Steed, and the General Manager of Sing's in Orlando are the norm, I'm just going to have to get you a secretary now, aren't I young man?" She paused and then smiled.

"Yes!" I jumped up and gave her a big hug.

"They all want you back tomorrow for second interviews!" she said, rubbing my head. "My boy is gonna be something in this world, I can feel it."

We celebrated for a couple of minutes and my mother said, "Why don't you go call that girl you're spending all that time with and let her know. I'm sure she'll be very proud of you."

"Good idea Ma, just give me a few minutes, I'll be right back." I dashed up to my room and called Karen with the good news. She was extremely happy for me, and said she would strongly consider the job at The Four Seasons in Boston if she got it. Since Chef William Steed of The Moon Room had called me, I told her I would think hard about Boston, which would also keep me closer to my family. While I was on the phone, my father had gotten home and my mother told him the good news.

"Congratulations boy, I heard all the jobs you wanted are interested in you. That's great, son," my father said with pride.

"Thanks Dad, that means a lot to me," I said, shaking his hand.

"So what are you going to do, are you leaning towards one in particular?"

"Well, Karen is thinking hard about Boston, so I'll have to re-interview tomorrow and see if that's the one I like. It is the best title for sure and they have a very well known chef, I guess we'll wait and see."

"When are we gonna meet this Karen?" my mother asked.

"Soon, I promise," I said.

"She sounds very lovely Jackson. She is always polite on the phone. Is she a keeper?" she asked.

"I think so Ma, I really like her," I replied.

"Well good for you honey, I've never seen you so happy so she must be doing something right."

"Thanks Ma, she is." I kissed my mother on her cheek and said, "I love you guys, I'm going to bed."

"No supper?" my mother asked.

"No, Karen and I just ate. I've got a big day tomorrow, I need some rest."

"All right honey, here are the numbers to call in the morning. We love you, baby," my mother said.

"Yeah, good work Jack," my father said.

"Thanks guys, see you in the morning," I said as I headed up to sleep. Tomorrow would be another big day.

CHAPTER 12

BILLY STEED

Living at home with my parents had its ups and down. The 30-minute ride to school was generally a down, but on this day it gave me time to rehearse what I would say and how I would respond to any line of questioning. I always did my best to play it cool, but I had butterflies for the first time I could remember in a while. Walking into the library that morning I intended to focus on a few specific places, one of which was The Moon Room, mainly because of 29-year-old chef William Steed. He was a well respected, James Beard nominated 1994 CIA graduate. He'd worked in both New York and Las Vegas before landing the executive chef position at Time, a cutting-edge restaurant that boomed for the three years of his reign until The Moon Room opened. The Moon Room was a happening night spot with a domed glass ceiling, a blue-illuminated back bar and black floors with blue and gray walls that just screamed night life. The food was praised from the get-go, and was awarded both "best new restaurant" and "best night life" by the *Boston Globe* and *Boston Magazine* in 1997.

My first appointment was with Chef Steed so I was a little anxious. As I approached the table he and another man stood up. "Jack, thanks for coming back, please take a seat." I sat on one side and they sat on the other, interrogation style.

"Thank you, Chef," I said as I sat down.

"Jack this is Charles Hayes, our general manager," William said.

"Jack, it's a pleasure to meet you. I understand you worked with Michael Roderick at the Dexter House, that's very impressive for someone as young as yourself. Tell me, is Chef Mikey as big a prick as everyone says he is?" Charles said to me with a quiet but sarcastic tone.

"Actually, he's a great guy and a great chef; I don't know where you heard that." I said in his defense.

"Oh well, I've only known him all my life," he said, cracking a smile. "You don't remember me do you Jack?" he asked, smiling harder. "I think Old Victor Payne single-handedly dropped the drinking age in New York just to please you. That's how much that guy likes you."

"How do you know that?" I asked.

"You had a lot to drink; I think you probably remember very little about that evening," he replied.

"You were at the party that night, weren't you? I do remember you, and you knew Mr. Payne pretty well if I recall correctly," I said excitedly.

"That's right. We speak regularly, and he wanted me to say hello to you today. He speaks very highly of you. He thinks you're the next Michael Roderick. I had a feeling I'd see you here today. Reaching for the branches of success at the age of what?" he asked.

"Eighteen, but technically you're not allowed to ask me that," I said. Chef Steed chuckled.

"Right you are, young man," Charles began. "Tell me, who else are you considering for your first big job as a CIA alumnus? Could it be Tishio, or maybe you want to do the tango with Mickey Mouse and Pluto down in sunny Orlando? Traditionally these interviews aren't so direct but Chef Steed and I are very busy. We wish to return to Boston and end this debauchery we call career day. So here's the only question I'm going to ask; your answer will either keep us talking or put us in Billy's Lincoln. Do you want to work for us?" he asked me directly.

With little or no time to think, I blurted out, "Yes. Tell me more." This was my kind of interview, hard, direct and to the point. Plus, Charles was a little annoying so the faster the better.

Chef Steed said, "You will receive no special treatment because of who you know. You will be taught by me, you will listen to what I tell you to do, and your input is only welcomed when it's requested. I've never taken on a sous chef with little to no experience; do not make me regret it."

"Yes, Chef. I won't let you down sir," I said sternly.

"Sir is what people call my father for God's sake; outside the kitchen call me Billy," Chef Steed said.

"Jack, your salary will be $700 a week and you'll receive half paid medical benefits," Charles started in. "This is our standard sous chef package. You help us grow you'll grow, simple right? Here's the catch, you have seven days to prove yourself. That's it. You're not up to par we have to let you go, you make it through that and the rest is up to you. Do you agree to these terms?" he said looking right at me.

"I not only agree, but I look forward to the challenges laid before me. I won't let you down," I said.

"Victor has an eye for talent, and he's got his eye on you. He told me that night at The Dexter House that he's looking forward to watching your career with great interest. You stay humble and focused and you'll do fine," Charles said, standing up. "Come on Billy, let's hit the road, we're done here."

"Thanks again Billy, thank you Charles, I look forward to joining the team," I said, shaking their hands.

"Talk to you soon Jack," Chef said, walking away.

I was blown away. I just landed the sous chef job at Boston's hottest restaurant. Could this really be happening? I gave a little fist pump to myself and smiled though I tried to hide it. Not only was I beyond excited about the job, I couldn't believe Victor still had me in mind! I had talked about him so many times to Karen, she was going to die when she heard all of this! I looked for her but she wasn't there. With complete jubilation in my step I headed out to find her. As I exited the library I noticed a couple of students running quickly toward the dorms. Without thinking much about it, I headed over that way and as I did, I saw siren lights flashing, an ambulance and police cars. I upped my pace, but others were running faster than me. As I got closer, I saw a stretcher being wheeled out of Karen's building. The body was covered in a white sheet and I totally freaked out. I dropped my files with no regard and raced over there. It was a quick run but all I could think about was Karen, I was praying she was fine, what the fuck was going on? As I got closer I saw Molly holding Karen, the two of them crying profusely. I was so relieved to see her but I was flabbergasted as to what was going on.

"What the hell happened?" I said, racing up to them and paJacking.

Karen let go of Molly and grabbed me. "Karen, what the hell happened, baby?" I asked, wiping her tears. She was hysterical.

"Tom killed himself," Molly said, rubbing Karen's back.

"What.....Holy shit.......Holy shit.......Oh my God........" I said, starting to cry. "What the hell.....Fuck!" I screamed. "NO! TOMMY! WHY!" I fell to the ground and was shaking. Karen was crying, and Molly started crying harder and fell to her knees. Other classmates arrived; Brad grabbed Molly on the ground and held her, and then Karen and I grabbed them. All of us just lay in each other's arms, and soon others joined in. It was the worst moment of my life; I had never felt so empty.

"What the fuck, who found him?" I asked in a state of shock but trying to compose myself to the enormity of the situation.

"It was Justin. He was lying dead in his bed when he did, pills all around him. Justin said his tongue was hanging out and he was sheet white, he said he knew he was dead the second he saw him. He's totally freaked out right now."

"Did anyone know, I mean, did he say...." I was trying to think but I couldn't. I don't think I even understood what was going on. I just sat there and listened. Listened to the cries of my classmates, the sounds of the emergency workers' walkie-talkies, and above all, the silence that screamed around it all. It was chilling. I'd been with him the night before, I mean just fucking with him and he hadn't said a thing! I guess I was blind, even though he had told Karen about this, I didn't even remotely see it coming.

I held Karen as she buried her face in my chest. She wasn't watching what was happening around her but I was. I saw them wheel Tom to the back of the ambulance, I saw them get ready to load him in, I saw his hand fall down below the sheet as they did, his lifeless hand just hanging there. I even saw them slam the door shut and pat the back of the ambulance to signal to the driver. After they pulled away with my friend's body, Karen held me tight and said, "Take me away from here Jack, get me away."

"OK Karen, come with me."

I picked her up and she gained her composure. Most of the emergency vehicles were starting to leave, but two police cars remained behind so the officers could ask questions. Justin was sitting on a bench mortified, just trying to answer them. No one was closer to Tom than we were, but everyone looked stunned and just blasted by the scene. I had to get Karen out of there. I had to get out of there.

We went to my parents' house in Pleasant Valley. They hadn't yet met Karen, the timing couldn't be worse, but I thought it would be the best place for her. It was a quiet ride there. No radio, no talking, an occasional deep breath, but that was all. We held hands the whole way.

We pulled up to my house and my father was mowing the lawn, which he practically did every two days. He stopped the mower when he saw my car pulling up. Karen got out of the car, distraught, and my father knew that something was up.

"Hey guys, everything OK?" he asked in a quiet way.

"Dad, this is Karen," I said glumly.

"Nice to meet you sweetheart, is everything OK?" he asked putting his arm around her.

"Mom inside?" I asked. I was a little more collected than Karen.

"Yeah, sure Jack. Linda come out here!" he screamed. "What's going on, son? Did you guys not get the jobs you wanted?"

My mother was walking over to us. "Dad, my friend Tom just committed suicide."

"Oh my God," he said, "I'm so sorry guys." He gave me a hug.

"Jackie what happened baby?" my mother asked, very concerned.

"Mom," I paused and hugged her, "my friend just killed himself," I said as Karen started to cry again. My father put his arm around her as I hugged my mother.

"Who baby, who killed himself?"

"My friend Tom, you know Tom from school, he's dead, and he killed himself." I repeated in total disbelief.

"Jack, I don't even know what to say. You must be Karen, are you all right honey?" my mother asked.

"I'll be OK. Thank you Mrs. Cahill."

"Come inside kids, we'll sit down," my mother said.

"Yeah that sounds good," I said glumly. I took a deep breath and took Karen's hand and escorted her inside. We sat and spoke to my parents at our kitchen table for a few hours. Karen apologized for meeting under these conditions. My parents were loving and considerate and treated her as if she were their own daughter. Finally, my mother and father headed upstairs for bed around 9pm. They kissed and hugged both of us. Karen and I poured some wine and went outside to sit on my folks' back porch, overlooking their beautiful garden and lake. It was a perfect place to get away from our troubles and talk.

"I hate it all," Karen said.

"Hate what love?"

"This. Not this right here, but this. Our lives are full of such joy. Your family is so amazing, our relationship is amazing, our education is amazing, and we have so much to be thankful for. How could someone close to us have so little?" she asked, staring off into the trees.

"I don't know baby, I have no idea, everyone is different I guess. He was different. Maybe he'd had enough of this life. I wish him well and will pray for him," I responded. "Me, I'm anxious to see what comes next in life, each day gets better for me. I took the job in Boston today."

"At The Moon Room?" she asked, cracking a smile.

"Yeah, they offered me a salary and the sous chef position," I said, looking at her.

"That's unbelievable Jack, why didn't you say something. I'm so proud of you," she said, hugging me.

"I figured I'd wait to tell you, considering the circumstances."

"Is this wrong?" she asked, pulling back. "Should we be happy right know? What are we supposed to be doing?"

"This. Living. That's our choice. I choose to live. Nothing will change that, and I choose to do that with you," I said, kissing her and rubbing foreheads.

"I love you Jack," she said softly, rubbing the back of my head and looking deeply into my eyes.

"I love you too Karen. More than you could possibly know," I replied, rubbing her hand and kissing her lips.

She pulled back slightly, smiled brightly and said, "I know you do, and that means more to me then you could believe."

CHAPTER 13

HERE WITHOUT YOU

Things were slightly derailed over the next few weeks and the timing couldn't have been worse. Tom's funeral was just awful; it gave everyone some closure, but we all still wondered what happened. He didn't actually leave a note, so there was just a lot of speculation, which I tried to stay out of. Hindsight is always 20/20, so in retrospect I guess there were signs that I had been too naive to see. I had some guilt about things I had done, but mainly I just felt sorry for him. Could I have helped? Could I have changed things? If I'd paid more attention, would he still be here? The memory of his face as we said goodbye after our last encounter will forever be tattooed in my mind.

The mood was different around campus, but we still had our lives to live. Rumors were flying, and broaching the topic was awkward whether you were praising him or condemning his death. I always stood up for him and tried to change the subject when it was mentioned; he was my friend and I missed him, but I was going forward and I needed to stay focused.

Karen had been struggling with the job search. She was rejected from The Four Seasons. She did eventually get a job offer as a link cook at The Harbor Side in Boston, though it wasn't exactly what she was looking for. She still wanted to move there and keep trying for The Four Seasons or anything that fit her interest, but her main reason for wanting to move to Boston was to be with me. I think she was starting to doubt her love for the kitchen and wanted to be involved with the business, but she wasn't sure in what capacity. We found a nice little apartment in Cambridge and I was eager to get there. Our place had some furnishings and the rest we planned to acquire as we went, a plan Karen was cool with. She had a few small things as well in her dorm that she wanted to take. Her dorm was a fairly easy pack, laundry and a few belongings, no real heavy lifting.

"Now how come I haven't seen these before?" Her laundry basket was right in front of me, and I pulled out a pair of very sexy, pink lacy panties.

She grabbed them from me. "Give me those!" she joked as she pulled them away slowly. "You want me to model them for you now?" she asked in a sexy way but with hint of sarcasm. We had been drinking white wine while packing and having fun for the first time in weeks.

"I'd be a fool to say no," I said, kind of getting turned on.

"Fine." She took them and put them on her head. "How do I look?" We were loose and happy and enjoying our remaining precious time on campus.

"Only you could make that hot!" I said, laughing out loud.

She took them off her head and toned down the laughter, "Seriously Jack, Boston in days! I mean what a journey it's been; did you ever think we'd be here?"

Sipping my wine I replied, "Honestly, yes I did. I can say with a total clean conscience that I did. I loved you from the minute I laid eyes on you."

"Shut up!" she screamed. She knew I meant it, but was being modest.

"I'm serious, Karen. I'm on the edge of my seat; I can't wait for our next chapter, away from here, away from everything, just us and a new start. It just feels right to me," I said, folding her CIA sweatshirt.

"Me too Jack, it feels very right," she said, happily packing away. "And you can love me even as a line cook?"

"Are you kidding? Have you seen how good you look in chef pants?" I said smiling, but totally wasn't kidding;

she did look sexy in her chef whites and it always turned me on.

She blushed and said, "Well, thank you, but I'm serious. I mean here you are, five years younger than me and already off to the races as a sous chef in a big pond like Boston, when I can't seem to get anyone to pay attention to me or take me seriously. What am I doing wrong?" she said, putting down the pants she was folding and grabbing her wine glass. She took a sip and said, "Is it me?"

"Totally not Karen, it's just a few places haven't worked out. You're plenty talented, smart, funny, easygoing, and personable. You have everything going for you. You'll see, you're going to be great baby, I have no doubt," I said, looking her in the eye to give her confidence. Frankly though, no matter how much I loved her, I wasn't totally confident. She seemed ambivalent about her future and I think it was starting to reflect in her demeanor, not with me but in general.

"Thank you Jack, you always know how to calm me down," she said, smiling at me.

"Anytime baby. Now enough pouty-pussing, we've got a party to get to!" I said, changing the mood.

With graduation the following day, Brad wanted to throw one last party before it was all over. We were so excited to be done with school, but in a bittersweet kind of way. In twelve hours we'd receive our medals and diplomas and be done. I helped finish packing and gave her a kiss, told her that I loved her, and headed home to get dressed for Brad's party.

At home I got ready to party. I spoke to my folks who expressed such pride in me. The next day at almost 19 years old I would graduate the youngest in my class, and in the top percentile. I was on top of the world. I smoked a joint on my way to the party just to get things going. When I got there I saw Karen and Molly sitting on the front porch. They had drinks in their hands, but looked pretty serious. I hopped out of my car, very excited to see them.

"Ladies ladies ladies, how are you on this fine evening! Molly you look ravishing as always, and my love, I don't have words." I was a little stoned and acting goofy. As I approached, Molly stood up without saying a word and went inside, rubbing Karen's back as she walked away.

"What's the matter honey?" I asked.

"You slept with Molly?" she asked looking up at me in tears.

"What?! She told you that?" I knew I was screwed.

"How could you not tell me that, Jack?" She screamed and hit me in the arm.

"That was before us," I said.

"You still should have told me! I mean, what else haven't you told me?"

"Nothing honey, all right, I did do that, but I was fucked up, I mean I thought you were sleeping with Tom and I was sitting in your room like a fool. I got drunk, went by her room to talk, and something happened," I said, attempting to calm her.

"You mean the night, the night that I was calming him down so he didn't KILL HIMSELF!" she screamed. "The night we've based everything on, the night we've talked about so many times, how could you leave out such a major detail!"

"I didn't think it was relevant," I said. Big mistake.

"Relevant? Relevant? Everything is relevant, Jack! I'm moving my life around yours, everything is fucking relevant!" she yelled.

"All right baby, calm down, I'm sorry," I said, attempting to touch her but she fought me off.

"Do not tell me to calm down," she said angrily. "It's not the fact that you did it, it's that you hid it from me."

"Karen, our lives are based around a lot more than some night you talked to Tom as I got drunk. What about the times we were together and you went home to Tom afterward? You don't think I felt pain? I'll bet there are guys you slept with before we met; you never volunteered that information, it's just not something you do. If you had asked I would have told you the truth," I responded.

"All right fine! Did you ever kill anyone, have you ever slept with my mother, uh, did you ever jump out of bed and fucking fly to school!?" she screamed. Karen rarely swore. "I thought some things were obvious, I guess not."

"Karen, it was over a year ago, we weren't together. You guys are friends; I didn't want to hurt that."

"Well, instead you've hurt me Jack. You hurt me, and that's something I thought could never happen. I never thought you could do that, in fact I was basing my life around it. I can't go to Boston with you; I can't even see you anymore."

"What? Karen you're being ridiculous, it's not a big deal," I begged.

"If you believe that, you don't know me at all." She hugged me and gave me a kiss on my cheek. "I love you Jack Cahill, you'll just have to conquer the world without me." She turned and ran away.

"Well go on then!" I screamed. Stunned, I took a seat on Brad's porch. A million thoughts ran through my mind. *Go upstairs and raise hell on Molly, chase after Karen to see if I can stop this, go have fun at the party the night before graduation.* Instead I just sat there. I heard the door open behind me. It was Molly, who looked at me in silence. I looked back with a scowl. I wanted to kill her, but instead I just turned and walked away. She called out, "Where's Karen?" as I approached my car.

"Gone," I said with my back to her. I got into my car and drove away. I felt like I just got punched in my stomach.

I loved that school, it meant so much to me and so did the people who were in it. I loved Karen with all my heart, but maybe given everything that had happened in the last two years, it was for the best. I wanted her with me, I wanted her by my side, I was head over heels in love with her, but as I drove away that night—maybe even in a state of shock—I thought for a moment that maybe this was right. I had been alone in New York, I could be alone again. I had a job to get to. That was always the most important thing to me, I couldn't let anything blind me of that.

Graduation day was hard. It was meant to be full of joy and promise, but instead it was dismal and cold. Karen and I didn't speak. Her family, with whom I had spoken on the phone but had never met in person were all in attendance. She looked broken the whole day. Nothing could have broken my parents' spirits, though, as they cheered for me when my name was called louder then anyone. I smiled at them as I walked across stage to receive my graduation medal. When President Ferdinand Metz put my medal on

I shook his hand and waved to my family. They were so proud.

The post-ceremony dinner was short, and I ate quickly with my sister and my parents. I've always wished that day had been more storybook, but I wasn't that lucky. When I was younger, my friends and I would stare at girls as beautiful as Karen, and only wish. Now I'd had one who wasn't only beautiful, but the kindest, sweetest soul I had known, and I had to let her go. I could have said something, tried harder, offered a clearer explanation, but I didn't. I watched her from across the room as she mustered up smiles and hugs for friends, and so did I. There were many tearful goodbyes that day, great friends who could never be replaced. The dining room at Roth Hall was filled with pride that day, and I shared in that pride, but truthfully, now, I just wanted to be done. School had been amazing but it had also knocked the wind out of me. I was ready to move on, full of mixed emotions but ready. While gazing at it all I heard my mother say, "You ready to go Jack?"

I enjoyed one last look around. I took a second to smile, to look at my friends smiling around me. I spent just a few seconds to let it all sink in and said with confidence, "Yes I am ma, yes I am."

With graduation behind me I wanted to waste no time. I had agreed to start at The Moon Room three days later and I'm glad that I did. I needed to get there; I needed to be in a kitchen and to be busy. There I was in control, something as of late I didn't feel that I was. When I arrived at my new place in Cambridge, my new landlord was a little taken back by the fact that I was moving in alone. "I tought de' was s'posd to be some broad livin' wich you?" he said gruffly.

"Yeah, that's not the case anymore. Here's the first and last months rent plus deposit you requested." I handed him $2100.

"You can pay this every month?" he asked.

"It's really not a problem."

"OK. But the first time it becomes a problem, you and I are chatting, boy." He smelled like cabbage and spit when he talked.

"You won't have to worry about me."

"OK Cahill, we'll see you on the first," he said as he handed me the keys and left.

I opened the door to the apartment Karen and I had chosen. "I'm here," I said aloud as I dropped my bags. There was a tiny balcony through the bedroom window and you could make out a partial view of Boston's downtown from it. I noticed a couple of beat-up old lawn chairs out there, so I grabbed a bottle of wine and my smokes and hopped out. The whirlwind of life was on the top of my mind, and finally, after days and months of the non-stop rollercoaster ride, I heard silence. The silence was almost more alarming than the chaos had been, as I sat and listened to the city noise, alone with my thoughts for the first time in a long time I just took a deep breath and sat back. Everything was running through my head as I sipped on a great bottle of cabernet. Most of my thoughts circled back to Karen, but I tried to fight them off and keep my mind where it needed to be—and that was on work. The next day was a huge day, and I had to keep that directly in the center of the radar screen. It was hard; her face kept popping into the back of my head, especially the more I drank. I felt buzzed and had smoked about a pack of cigarettes, so I stumbled back through the window and abruptly stopped. I looked around at my new place, I rubbed my eyes out of fatigue and my stupor, and headed to bed. As I dug out a pair of shorts and a tee shirt from my bag to sleep in I came across a picture of Karen. I stared at it for a minute and became full of emotion but didn't let it come to the surface. Sighing, I put it down, hit the lights and went to sleep.

CHAPTER 14

ELROY JETSON

The next morning I was awoken by the sound of sirens in the background and the sun shining through my window. Eager and energetic but a little hung-over, I took a quick shower, threw my chef whites into my backpack, grabbed my knife bag, and headed out. It was time to rise to the challenge.

"Good morning Chef," I said as I walked into the kitchen for my first day.

"Good morning Jack, nice to have you with us. We have a lot to do before service starts so suit up quick," Chef said as I walked in.

"Yes Chef," I said. "Where do I do that?"

"Down the hall there's a changing room. You brought your own suit, right?"

"Of course, I'll be right out." I dressed quickly, grabbed my blade, and headed towards Billy.

"Chef, where shall I begin?" I asked.

"Well let me give you a tour of the place first Jack. Over here is the—"

"Thank you Chef, but I paid attention on my way in. I've got my knife, put me to work, I gave myself the tour already."

He paused, "Very well. Let's get you right to work then, shall we? I need 20 gallons of split pea soup." He turned around and grabbed a three ring binder from behind him. "The recipe is right in there, any questions I'll be on the line." He turned to leave, but paused and said, "You have made it before, yes?"

"Yes of course, Chef," I replied. He kept on walking. The kitchen was divided into two parts: a main line that was open to the dining room, and a rear prep kitchen that was small and cramped. Cookbooks lined the shelves with spices and various culinary tools. The dish area was small, and the walk-in cooler was even smaller. The line itself was brand new complete with state-of-the-art stainless steel equipment, copper pans and was spotless from top to bottom. It was a straight line, exposed to the dining room with an expediting station on the other side. It looked small, considering how much volume the restaurant did, but it was very efficient.

I got to work on my split pea soup, showing myself around the coolers and storage spaces as I went. Chef Bill was working around the kitchen, no doubt keeping a close eye on everything I was doing, though he looked busy. I tried my hardest not to bother him and to find my own way around. My attitude was always the fewer questions you need to ask, the better. I felt it showed greater independence, an attribute of every great chef. I assembled my soup quickly, but it had to cook for a couple of hours before I could purée it. Once it was simmering, I noticed the daily produce order was being delivered. I approached the deliveryman and took the invoice, then began to check in the product for quantities, quality, short ships and out of stock items. Once I had completed it, I brought the invoice over to Chef Billy to verify it was what he ordered. He glanced at it briefly and said, "Did you check everything?"

"Yes Chef, everything is here."

"All right, sign it in, kid."

I signed it and sent the deliveryman on his way. Chef approached me, "On an average day we get anywhere from six to thirteen different deliveries. It is your responsibility to ensure all product that is ordered is here and up to par. We do about six million dollars in sales a year here, and we purchase about two million to do it. Small percents matter, pounds missing, poor quality, shelf life, they add up to thousands of dollars, so do a good job, OK Jack?"

"I can do that." I headed back to the kitchen to check my soup, gave it a quick stir, and headed back to the cooler to put the delivery away, which took about 20 minutes. After I had completed it, another one came in and while I was putting that away, two more came in. This went on all day, receiving product and stirring soup. Line cooks showed up and introduced themselves—it seemed like a nice crew. I didn't really have time to meet them though; I was busy organizing the walk-in all day. I had no idea why it was me doing it though; it almost looked like nobody did it at all, or else they had no interest in stopping me from doing it. We received more than $5,000 in product that day and I was in charge of it all on my first day.

Once all was said and done in the cooler, I pureed my soup, poured it into five-gallon buckets, and cooled it down in sink bays full of ice. Chef had me do a few other tasks but it felt like busy work, either that or he wasn't really paying attention to what I was doing at all. Before I knew it five o'clock was here and everyone was getting ready for dinner service. Chef was out front with Charles; they were talking so I just stood politely until they were finished. Charles noticed me standing there and turned. "Can I help you?" he said rudely.

"Hi Charles, it's nice to see you again, I'm just waiting to talk to Chef, no rush."

"This doesn't concern you, go back to the kitchen. Chef will be with you later." He turned back to Billy and started to talk again. Shocked by his rudeness, I turned and walked back to the kitchen. My blood was boiling but I humbly left. What was going on at this place?

Distracted and confused, I looked for something to do. I walked up and down the line and peeked at what the cooks were doing. A grill cook turned and acknowledged me, saying, "What was your name again?" He was an older guy, probably about 40.

"I'm Jack, I'm the new sous chef here, what was your name again?"

"If you're the new sous here, I'm fucking Abe Lincoln," he said, laughing at me. "Hey Mario, you meet our new sous yet?" he yelled, laughing. Mario came over. "Hey Mario, meet our new sous, this is Elroy Jetson. Elroy, this is Mario." Mario had a good laugh about it. I couldn't show them it was getting to me.

"Are you done yet?" I asked.

"Sorry Elroy, that was a good one though. Did I tell you that I was running for president next month, hope I win," he said, crossing his fingers and laughing with a deep smokers laugh.

"What's your name?" I asked him.

"None of your business kid," he said, slowing down on his laughter.

"Your name?" I said again. I noticed Chef rounded the corner and stopped to listen.

"Alan, but these guys call me Hack," he said.

"Well Hack, I'll tell you what I'm gonna do here. I'll bet you that I can run the grill tonight, no assistance, no re-fires, no long tickets, no problems at all. All I'll need from you is how the Chef likes each dish plated, one time. After you show me once you can step aside and watch me cook. End of the night, I keep my word you clean the station and I drink. I have one problem, just one, even a steak temperature, I clean and buy you as many drinks as you can handle, and by the looks of things you can hold a fair amount," I said confidently.

"You have ID for drinks boy?" he said, stepping towards me.

"I'll drink soda. We have a deal Hack?" I said, stepping towards him.

"Doesn't matter how old you are, you won't do it. Even Chef has a re-fire sometimes. Yeah, I'll let you scrub my station punk, and after that I'll let Chef deal with you. My new sous chef, I wonder what I'll learn from you. Maybe how to pop the zits on my fat hairy ass, or maybe I'll let you do it for me," he said, turning away. "I'm going for a smoke."

"Respect," I whispered to myself, taking a deep breath. Chef made eye contact with me and then turned away. He didn't really make an expression regarding what just happened; I couldn't tell if he respected me for standing up for myself or was disappointed that I was upsetting the herd. The last thing I wanted to do was to be gung ho and come in guns blazing. I knew I was younger than anyone there, and I knew I had less experience then them too, but I had confidence in my abilities. For the first time I felt strong and was starting to believe what people were saying about me. Maybe I did have something special, maybe I was a true prospect, maybe I could be bigger than them all, bigger than Billy, bigger than Michael. None of that mattered now, now it was all about backing up what just happened. Now it was all about cooking.

When I worked the Garde Manger station at the Dexter House, the tickets came in so fast and furious right from the get-go. Here, though, things started much later in the evening. We didn't get cranking until about 8pm but we stayed busy right up to midnight. As the early dishes started coming in, Hack was breathing down my neck, right over my shoulder. He stank like dried-up whiskey and one too many smokes. He was so close I could practically feel his

5 o'clock shadow, which looked more like a 10 o'clock shadow. I knew he wanted me to fail, but he kept his word and showed me how to plate every single dish the way Chef wanted it to be plated. He explained with great detail, no matter what a jerk I thought he was; I could see he at least cared about food, which gave some respect for him. As he explained each dish, he never made eye contact with me; he looked straight at the food. His hands were thick, with such fat fingers that he could barely pick the fresh live herbs we used for garnish, but somehow his dishes looked great.

Once we got going the whole place was alive. Chef Billy handled the situation masterfully, with total control and great calm, leaving no doubt that he knew what he was doing. Servers hustled in and out, and he gave them clear commanding instructions with surgical precision. He demanded things go his way and so they did; his orders were followed and no one stepped out of line. Issues mostly came from servers or from a line cook, but halfway through service no one had made any mistakes, including me.

"Pick up table 30, grill two lamb racks, one rare, one medium well, sauté pick up two chickens, fry pick up one pomme soufflé," Chef said firmly.

"Two lambs, one rare, one medium well," I repeated. In Billy's kitchen everyone did a call back, every time, no questions. If you didn't, he assumed you did not hear his order, which did happen sometimes due to heavy pans clanking and loud hood vents working in your ears. You had to pay attention, because callbacks were a major part of Chef Billy's system and no one went against what he said.

"Two chickens heard," Mario said.

"One pomme soufflé, Chef," Travis said. Travis was a mangy-looking guy with long black hair tied up into a short pony tail, thick black glasses, a long scraggly goatee, and tattoos on his forearms. For a guy who looked a little rough, he sure could hold his own.

Chef put the table together, handed the dishes to Jason, one of our best servers, and told him what was what. I saw Chef hand him the rare lamb and tell him it was the medium well and vice versa. I wanted to correct him but I thought Jason, as well-seasoned as he was, would be able to tell the difference just by looking. He said, "Yes Chef," and hustled out of the kitchen.

Time was flying, tickets were fierce, and I could feel the energy of The Moon Room all the way back to the grill. I was in a total rhythm, and I even caught Hack whispering to Travis as Travis nodded with recognition—I knew they were talking about me. I kept my head down because Chef was keeping a close eye on me; I knew that if my personal vendetta jeopardized service it was going to be a major black Tom on my seven-day trial period.

"Grill pick up 4 sirloins all medium rare, sauté pick up one halibut, fry—" Chef's orders came to a halt. I picked my head up only to see Charles looking at me and whispering in Chef's ear. Chef threw a glance in my direction, nodded, and Charles left.

"—Fry pick up 2 frittes."

"Two frittes heard Chef!" Travis said like the mad man he was.

I was a little thrown off by their exchange but I regained my composure and shouted, "Four sirloins all mid-rare Chef!" I plated the sirloins and went on with the night.

Around 12:15am I put out my last dish. As I did, I threw down my towel and pumped my fist with satisfaction. I was so excited I couldn't contain myself; it was a perfect service, not one re-fire, over-season, too dry, too spicy, nothing! It wasn't the first time this had happened, but on a very busy night, to have a rookie not have any cooking issues was a huge accomplishment. I did it; I did what I set out to do.

"Grill, breakdown, all out, good job," Chef said routinely. Stations broke down as they completed.

Desserts were still going so we all cleaned up while they worked. Even though Hack had to clean my station, cleaning didn't technically begin until Chef's post-meal recap was complete. Chef always did post-meal, reviewing what happened, how it happened, and how we could do it better. He very much reminded me of Chef Roderick the way he never gave up on his efforts to improve. He was never fully satisfied and never settled.

"Dessert pick up 2 poached pears!" he said, knowing it was his last ticket. He didn't look remotely tired.

"Two pears," repeated Kim the pastry chef.

Four minutes later Kim said, "Two pears in the window Chef, all out!" Kim was very pretty and very quiet. She had sandy blonde hair and brown eyes, a thin waist and big hips and man she could move.

"Thank you Chef." Billy called Kim chef because pastry chefs are a unique breed. They're sort of like freelance hit men, they are part of the team but move independently and at their own pace. The good ones like Kim make their own hours and create their own dishes, as long as it fits with the concept of course. That was very much the relationship Kim and Chef had, except during service she listened to him. The only thing he insisted on was timely delivery of plated desserts and how she made them. "Great job!" he added.

"Thank you Chef," she repeated as she was already wiping down her station.

"Great job by everyone tonight, gather up for postmeal. Jason, I'll take a Guinness," he said, motioning his hand near his mouth like he was drinking an invisible beer.

"Yes Chef," he said quickly, moving towards the door. Chef grabbed his clipboard, unbuttoned his coat, laid it on the counter, and started talking as we were still gathering up. Everyone looked a little tired, everyone except him.

"Great service tonight, that's the way we need to do it all the time. Kim, your desserts were as pretty as you are," he said as she blushed, "but the delivery on those wild berry cobblers was a little slow, you need to shave 5 minutes off that pick-up time, that can't slow down our turns." She looked like she agreed and nodded. "Sauté, all fish looked great, chicken looked a little overcooked, let's pay a little more attention to it, wasn't your best stuff Mario," he said. Mario simply said, "Yes Chef," and Chef moved on. "Travis, A-plus man, you did have one pomme soufflé look a little flat but hey nobody's perfect," he joked.

"No, but I'm the next best thing to it," Travis said. Everyone laughed mildly.

"Grill team, Hack and Jack, spot on boys, the night was great. I haven't seen a service like that for a while. We did have a complaint on a lamb though; the customer ordered it rare and said it was medium. They didn't want to wait for another one so we just took it off the bill but watch those lambs; they can be tough to tell sometimes. Otherwise, great job by all, let's breakdown and get ready for another busy day tomorrow," he said, taking a small sip of his newly delivered beer. As he did he picked up his coat and headed for his office.

"Well Elroy, hope you have some space age system of cleaning up this line. By the way, you were right, I can drink a ton and I'm fucking thirsty tonight! Hope you brought your piggy bank; close don't get you no cigars!" he said, coughing while trying to laugh.

"What are you talking about; I put that out right, Che—" I stopped talking dead in my tracks.

"What were you saying? Maybe I need to clear out some of this ear wax to hear you Elroy?" he said, literally picking his ear.

"Nothing, you're right, I said no mistakes and I made one. Drink up Hack, drink up," I said, shaking my head. I knew Chef mixed that up, I saw it happen and should have said something—not even for my own selfish needs, but the guest left unhappy and hungry. I truly cared about that; that's why I do this, to impress people with my food. That's why all great chefs do it, at least the ones who shoot for perfection.

"Thanks, I will. I'll be across the street at the Hot House; feel free to come by with your allowance. I hope your mommy gave you enough," he laughed. "You're gonna need it." He strapped his filthy towel on my shoulder. I scraped it off and got to work.

Around 1:15 I finished. The dishwashers were still very hard at work, the bar at the Moon Room was still totally packed and alive, the mood was so great and the music was on full blast. Loving the scene but itching to settle up with Hack, I cleaned my knives, packed up my kit, and headed across the street.

"Hey Jack, wait up, you heading to the Hot House?" I turned and saw Jason running towards me. We only knew each other through the night's service; we were never actually introduced.

"I was going to; I'm Jack Cahill by the way," I said.

"Well *duh*!" he said flamboyantly. Jason was tall, thin and clean-cut. He was wearing a leather jacket, jeans, black shoes and his white waiter shirt. He was a really nice guy, gay as a blade and smart as they come.

"What do you mean by 'duh'?"

"Everyone knows who you are; they've been talking about you since Charles and Billy came back from New York! And, if I might add, rightfully so. You were *fabulous* tonight!" he said excitedly, patting me really hard on the back. He always sounded really excited.

"May I be so bold as to ask what they are saying?"

"Well, they say you come from New York City, you graduated the CIA, you worked at the Dexter House— which, if I may say, *yum*—and that you are the youngest sous chef we have ever had! And, at the expense of ratting him out, which I don't really care because he's a big fat slob anyway, the cook Alan, or Hook or whatever they call him, has not been such a big fan! I guess he thought he was going to be sous chef and POW, out pops you!!" he said, speaking really fast and energetically. My eyes were wide open as I listened and I was nodding so fast I got dizzy.

"Well I didn't come here to cause any trouble, I'm really just interested in doing my job and keeping it," I said, approaching the door to the Hot House.

"Psss….oh please, anyway!" he laughed. We stopped just outside before we went into the Hot House. "Billy knows you have it all over those guys, and they know it too. The restaurant is good, Billy is amazing, but the cooks can be as off as they smell some nights. This place can be a little disorganized behind the scenes, I can't tell you how many times I had to clean up Hack's mess! He sucks, you don't; he's aging, you're young; he's just jealous and Billy knows it. You play your cards right and hold your own, don't let that guy or any of them push you around. I haven't seen a night that smooth in a long time, you're going to be great for us!" he said, slapping me in the arm and smiling.

"Well, I appreciate the vote of confidence but I guess time will tell."

"It's told, now come on—let me buy you a drink," he said, opening the door for me.

"I'm only 19," I stated.

"Duh squared!" he said, laughing. "The bartender's my boyfriend, I think he'll let you in!"

I extended my arm. "After you," I said.

He pinched me on the cheek as he passed me, "God, if you were gay I would eat you alive!" he said, increasing the pitch of his voice.

"Well, you can start by buying me that drink," I joked. I looked up at the city for a second, looked across the street at The Moon Room, and the door closed behind me.

CHAPTER 15

THE HOT HOUSE

The Hot House Tavern was a very popular nightspot in Boston— an afterhours club that you could bring your own booze to. That wasn't common; in fact, that was a very hard license to obtain. In Boston, bars closed at 2am on the weekends, but The Hot House stayed open until 5am; you just had to have your own alcohol after 2am.

The House, as everyone called it, had customers from all walks of life, from businessmen to frat boys and it was always packed. The place was dimly lit with a square hardwood bar in the middle of the place. The walls were red, the trim was gold, and small candles were on every table that surrounded the bar. It wasn't a huge place but it was very popular, especially with restaurant people because of the late hour. I saw Hack at the bar, sitting with Mario, the two of them hunched over talking. There were a couple of empty shot glasses in front of them and Hack was guzzling a Bud Lite. He turned and looked right at me, but he looked so drunk that he didn't even recognize me.

"Last call guys," all three bartenders starting shouting. The girl with red hair wearing a black tank top, tight black jeans, and entirely too much make-up was ringing a large brass bell. "Last fucking call so pay those tabs you deadbeats and tip the shit out of me or you won't see these again!" she said grabbing her breasts and shaking them up and down. The guys went crazy for it and screamed, but Jason just rolled his eyes. She was very 80s in her style.

"Well, last call, maybe I'll just pass. I don't want to fight that mob for a beer; I think I'll just call it a night."

"Don't be silly, I have a locker here with some yummy reds in it! I'll get us a few glasses. I'm sure Chef will be over soon; his locker has even better juice then mine!" he said, waving to the bartender. The bartender smiled, Jason stuck two fingers in the air and he pulled out two glasses. "That's Jay, my boyfriend!" he said, still looking at him. "Yes I know, Jason and Jay is so gay but hey, fuck it, you only live once! Now, what are you in the mood for, stud?" he asked. "I've got a great bottle of pinot noir in there."

"Pinot would be great," I said, still absorbing the scene and watching the door waiting for Chef to come in. I was excited to hear he was coming, and anxious to hear what he had to say about the night. Jason came back quickly with the bottle of wine. "Super delicious!" he said as he presented the bottle to me.

"That is a great bottle." It was a Stags' Leap 1994; most of my wine knowledge came from what I learned at the CIA and my osmosis from Victor. I had never actually tasted this wine but I tried to play it cool.

"So, you cook," he said, pouring me a glass. We were lucky to have gotten a table in the still very busy bar. "You clean; I know this because your station looked spic-n-span-erific tonight, and you're a young talented sous chef at Boston's hottest restaurant. How are you single again?" he said as he placed down the bottle. "Plus you are h-o-t; you've got some explaining to do mister!"

"So do you, sir." It was Jay the bartender, now dressed in regular clothes and sitting down with us. "You're not supposed to be telling anyone they're hot but me, even if he really is!" he joked lightheartedly. They were a quirky little couple.

"Oh stop it, you know I'm only kidding. Jay, this is Jack Cahill, he's the new sous chef across the street. Look at him, isn't he fabulous!" he said brushing my shoulder.

"Oh, so you're the one I've been hearing about all night," he said, picking up his glass and pointing at me.

"You've got quite the fan club already," he said as he flicked his head towards Hack.

"Well, I can't help it if people want to talk about me. If they don't have anything better to discuss then be my guest."

"From what they said you can certainly hold your own. They were calling you the boy wonder, and the drunker they got, the more jealous they sounded." He leaned in and whispered, "I'll spare you from all the other wonderful things they had to say about you." He laughed as he said it.

"Oh please, those guys couldn't beat a four-year-old with an Easy Bake Oven in a cook off! How do you think Alan got his nickname, Hack; he's so dense he thinks it's a compliment. And Mario, he's lucky Chef has kept him around this long. His only beef would be now that you're here Bill might just wipe his hands clean of that one. They're bad for us; Hack couldn't do what you did tonight if his life depended on it," Jason said, already finishing his first glass. I had barely even had a sip.

"He might say otherwise," I said smoothly.

"Duh trice! He would say a lot of things otherwise. They're yesterday's news Jack, and they know it," Jason added, topping off my full glass.

"Well thank you, that means a lot," I added.

"So, no question dodging, who's the lady in your life?" Jason said. The two of them leaned forward, put their hands to their faces and their elbows on their knees with interest.

"Well . . .," I started to explain. Just then Mambo No. 5 came on the radio and Jason jumped up with great interest.

"Oh my God, hold that thought—Jay, we HAVE to dance to this!" he said, pulling him out of his chair.

Jay sighed. "Fine, but just one song tonight, you queen," he said flatly. He slowly sauntered behind a very excited Jason to the dance floor.

As he did, I felt my night had come to an end. This was fun, a little wine with Jason, but I didn't want to overstay my welcome; besides, watching them happy and dancing made my mind drift as it usually did. I knew I owed Hack for his drinks so I went to the counter and threw a hundred dollar bill on it right in front of him.

"Hey," he said, dazed. I didn't even acknowledge his drunken grunt, I just turned and left. As I walked out the door Chef Billy was just arriving with a sexy young waitress from The Moon Room. "Hey!" he said, surprised to see me. "What's up man, what the fuck are you doing here?" I could tell he'd had a few drinks.

"Nothing Chef, just having a quick one and heading home, it's a long way back to Cambridge," I said stiffly.

"Well, you may recognize Natalie, and this is her friend Candace. Ladies, meet the great Jack Cahill, my new sous chef from New York," he said, letting go of Natalie's hand and putting his arm around me proudly.

"It's nice to meet you ladies," I said, keeping my head low trying not to get involved.

"New chef huh?" Candace said, "You must be pretty talented to be working with Will Steed." I'd never heard anyone call him Will before. The girls were all over him and looking me up and down. Chefs can attract quite a following, there's something about it; I don't know if it's being in command, the cooking, the uniform, or something else, but there is definitely something. Whatever it is, it was clear these two girls liked it.

"I wouldn't go that far but I do my best," I said, trying to be humble, like Chef Mike. Billy was a little more arrogant and outward about it; he enjoyed the rock star status a little bit more.

"Well, why don't we all grab a table and get to know each other a bit more, shall we?" he said, extending his arm towards an open table that was just being cleaned. Great table, right by the window, you could see a lot of Boston from there.

"I can't Chef but thank you, see you in the morning?" I said firmly, now making better eye contact.

"Oh, come on!" Candace said. "I want to discuss all of your talents." She moved her hand towards my face and I backed away. "Perhaps some other time," I said firmly and I headed to the door. Billy said, "Take a seat girls, I'll be right back." I could hear him as the door closed behind me.

"Jack!" he shouted, his voice echoing loudly through the nighttime streets. "Jack, wait up!" I stopped.

"You OK man?" he asked.

"I'm good Chef thanks, just have a lot on my mind."

"I know the feeling. You really were great tonight, I don't need seven days to see that. The job is yours. We have much to discuss, so let's meet as soon as you get in tomorrow to go over a game plan."

"I will be there of course, Chef. I'm flattered, thank you." And I was, but I was tired.

"You have a lot of talent in you. I'm gonna be the one who teaches you how to control it, no more bets, no more games, I'm gonna show you how to do it without needing to put out your chest so often. You will learn how to be a great chef, I will see to it," he said, flicking me in the belly. He was smiling and already heading back to the bar. "Sure you don't want to come back in? If not, I'll have to handle these two girls by myself!" he said, rocking back and forth like a boxer.

"Something tells me you won't have any problem with that," I said, forcing a smile.

"You know it bitch," he said. "Later bro, see you tomorrow morning!"

On the bus ride home I thought a lot about what he'd said. I knew he was good on the line but he did mix up my lamb racks. I knew he looked strong but he'd hired a weak team, or at least that was my opinion. *Billy Steed huh, is this the person I want to make me into a chef?* Was this the person I wanted to learn from, the person to mold me, or was he someone I was better than, someone I could take out, so I could make my own name? That was the question on my mind.

That thought kept me going until I got home to my cold, unpacked empty apartment. It was late and the place seemed so void of any warmth or feeling. I was very tired. It was 3am, and I just lay down and crashed.

CHAPTER 16

A CRACK IN THE ICE

On day two I went in with a whole new approach. Billy was on board, I felt great from the previous night's service, and with Jason's insider's perspective, I had all I needed after just one day to start making my impact felt.

"Elroy!" I heard immediately upon entering, "you're late! Mommy ground you for being out past curfew last night?" Hack said, elbowing his Siamese twin Mario in the ribs as the two of them laughed in perfect harmony. I was more than on time—I was 20 minutes early.

"Chef here?" I asked, ignoring their antics and looking over their shoulders trying to spot him.

"Yeah, he's here, and here's your change boy. I didn't ask for your money, just wanted what I had coming to me," he said, placing $30 on the counter. The bills were crumpled up and looked a little ripped.

"Thanks, and don't worry—you'll get what's coming to you soon enough," I said as I walked past them. I wasn't normally rude, but the hazing was starting to get on my nerves. I was already in my chef pants with my white T-shirt tucked in, and my knife kit was hanging over my shoulder.

"Cocky little bastard, we'll see who gets his," I heard him say as I walked away. I walked out into the dining room looking for Chef and saw him and Charles drinking coffee and laughing as I walked in. They were near the bar, just the two of them.

"Oh, there he is!" Billy said, noticing me as I approached. He was still smiling but his laughter slowed down.

"Morning Chef, Charles," I said. Charles gave me a look like I was interrupting, but it didn't look like work talk. Chef was staring at me too with a *what are you doing here* kind of look. "Did you want to meet this morning?" I asked, as he blankly looked at me.

"Owww! Sorry about that Jack, I'm behind schedule, I was tied up all morning!" he said breaking into laughter. Charles laughed too, like they were both in on the joke. "No matter Jack, start setting up middle and we'll catch up later," he said, shuffling me away.

"Yes Chef," I said in a softer, more confused tone. He didn't seem to think anything of it; as I turned, I heard him say, "So Chuck that's so funny, they both had me tied up and…." The sound drifted as I walked away. *What is with this guy?* I thought. No matter, I was back in one of Boston's best kitchen on day two, already setting up middle which was where Chef worked. I had never done it, nor been given any guidance as to how to do it, but I figured I'd seen what Chef did the night before so I could try to replicate it as best I could. I was quickly learning that Billy wasn't great with direction, but luckily I didn't need it.

Middle wasn't difficult to set up, but you had to be very specific. They called it middle because it was the center of the line, and each and every plate that left passed through it. It was the most important station of them all; each station was busy, but it was the middle that put it all together, sort of like the maestro of an orchestra. You needed to be very focused and detail-oriented at that station: the whole line was counting on you, your hand touched every dish, and although you may not have made each one you had a part in them all. Much of what you did was coordination, but you also garnished many as well. The set-up needed to be precise.

I had two major things to set up: Chef's ice well, which contained all the cold garnishes, and the hot holder that had most of the finishing sauces. It didn't seem like much, but I really wanted to impress Chef despite the fact that this day was rubbing me the wrong way. I blocked it all out and got to work.

"Hey Jack." It was Hack; I looked up at him a little startled because he had never used my real name before.

"Yeah Alan," I said looking back down at my work. I was very focused on the julienne rhubarb I was cutting for our duck entrée.

"I will hand it to you man, you did pretty good last night. I'm not saying I was impressed, but you held up well for a rookie. I just don't know what makes you think you could teach anyone here anything at your age. We know what the hell we're talking about and I just don't see how you could lead us. You may be a solid line cook, but do you really think you're a qualified sous chef? Why don't you go back to New York and give us a call in five years," he said, peeling garlic. I noticed he pressed his garlic too hard and left skin on it when he minced it, hence the name Hack, I guess.

"Stop slamming your knife like that," I said, looking up at him with my eyes but remained hunched over in my work. I always cut leaning over because I was so tall. As I did, I noticed Chef and Charles round the corner though I did not look in their direction. Hack did, though.

"Hey!" I said firmly. "Don't look at them; look at me when I'm talking to you." I stood up and grabbed the pan of already chopped garlic he had on his station. I turned it upside down and slammed it hard onto his cutting board. It made him jump.

"What the fuck is your problem!" he proclaimed, startled.

"My problem is you slam your knife so hard when you squish your garlic that you leave skin in each piece, see? Look, skin, skin," I was picking through the garlic I had dumped out, pulling out pieces with the tip of my knife. "There's goddamn skin all over this thing. You're so worried about me, my age, where I've been and what I can teach you, and you can't even peel garlic correctly. I would be willing to bet, Hack, if you can't even peel garlic—something I've been doing properly since I was 15—then I bet there's a lot you can't do. The purpose of *peeling* garlic is to remove the skin. Not just some of it, all of it! So from now on, no more fucking skin is to be left on "peeled" garlic! There, I just taught you something." I calmly picked up my knife, hunched over, and began cutting my rhubarb again. Hack looked at Chef, looked down at his garlic, and got back to work. Charles turned to Billy and said, quietly enough that I wasn't supposed to hear but I did, "This kid's either gonna be the best thing that's ever happened to us, or our biggest mistake to date." Chef nodded and walked over to me. "Chef Jack, how's our set-up?" Billy had just called me Chef, I got such a chill, and he'd done it for all to hear, too.

"Set-up is strong Chef, only a few last things to tie together," I responded, but didn't stop cutting.

"It looks good; we need double this for veal reduction, triple the thyme sprigs, a little more cinnamon oil, grab a few grapefruits, and you're missing mole sauce. I'll get going on a line walk and we'll finish this up together. Great set-up for your first time, you really do pay attention," he said much more seriously than earlier in the day.

"Yes Chef, thank you Chef," I said respectfully.

Chef did his line walk, which involved checking each station to see if it is ready for service. He checked to make sure there was enough product, that it was prepped correctly, seasoned right and held properly. He did this every night. This Billy was much different than the Billy I'd seen making jokes before, by the bar. He seemed much more focused and intense. He asked a few guys to make some changes but for the most part setup was right on. Chef was going out to do pre-meal; it was 4:15 and we were getting ready to open. He stopped by to see me before he headed out.

"Make those changes Jack, and let's be ready," he said, patting me on the chest.

"Yes sir," I said, already cutting my grapefruits. Chef gave me a half smile and headed out, but before he did he said, "You'll sit next to me and watch tonight, no cooking, just watching, something I should have had you do last night. Sorry about blowing off our meeting this morning, didn't mean to Jack, let's try again tomorrow. Looks like we have a lot to discuss."

"Yes Chef," I said proudly. I was excited about the quick momentum but it was service time so I stayed totally focused.

Service came hard and fast that night, even flatter seating, quicker turns and bigger parties. Chef maintained his level of focus, the crew held up well, and even Hack did OK with only four re-fires. I could see more and more why they called him Hack; his apron was filthy, his jacket became untucked and his station was disorganized, at least when he was busy. Being a chef is about much more than just cooking; it's a career where absolute organization is to be maintained at all times or things can spiral out of control quickly.

The last ticket was finishing up. "Pick up dessert table 32, 4 soufflés, 1 mousse, 1 cobbler, let's double time it guys and call it a day," Chef said with the same level of intensity that he called the first ticket. Kim was already pulling four perfectly timed soufflés out of the oven. She finished them all in about two minutes, calling back to Chef, "Table 32 in the window Chef."

"Thank you Kim, spot on as always," Chef said, handing them off to the server.

"Great job guys, break it down and drinks on me, A-plus everyone!" he said, folding his apron. He grabbed his clipboard and whispered to me in passing, "Make sure breakdown is done, grab a beer, and meet me in the office." He patted my shoulder as he walked away. He may have been hard to read, he may have seemed a little unpredictable, but he was my Chef, and after a night like that I was finally proud to call him that.

After most of the cooks had unbuttoned their coats, turned up the music and returned from their post-service smoke break, they smoothly broke down their stations. Breakdown was easy; I made sure my pans were changed and everything was cooled and stored properly. As the last of the cooks were finishing up and the floors were starting to get swept, I headed towards the office unannounced. The door was opened just a crack and I could hear Billy talking on the phone.

"Yes sir . . . yes I have been . . . you were right, he has incredible promise . . . I am too, sir . . . yes, I will keep you informed, once a week sir until he is ready . . . thank you sir, I look forward to seeing you soon." He hung up. I could see him leaning back in his chair and taking a deep breath as he looked up at the ceiling.

I knocked, "You wanted to see me Chef?"

"Yeah, come on in Jack," he said. "I just wanted to apologize about today, I didn't mean to blow you off. Life has a way of not always allowing you to do what you want to do, you know what I mean?"

"Of course Chef," I said softly.

"Sit down," he said pulling the other chair out in his very tiny, messy office. "We can skip coffee tomorrow, I'll just hit you with it now. I like you, a lot in fact, and you have the support of all of us, I'm sure you know that. What I don't know is if you are truly able to handle what lies in front of you."

"I can handle anything you give me in this kitchen Chef," I said with great confidence.

"I'm sure of that, or at least I feel like I am. However you have real opportunities to be much more than just that. I know the old man likes you—what he sees, though, I'm sorry to say I don't, at least not yet. I will say you can cook, you're tough, you're wicked comfortable and under control in a kitchen, but will you break? Will you snap? Can you handle the spotlight, the pressure of the publics' eye? That's what I don't see, at least not yet, but I will tell you Victor does. Being a Chef goes far beyond the grill, talented Chefs, Victor Payne Chefs have to be able to handle the pressures both in and out side the kitchen. There's a cold side of the grill Jack, and it can get pretty ugly very quickly. Victor thinks you have it, but he has been wrong before." He paused to sip his nearly empty beer.

"I have a job: to get you ready for the next thing, it's coming. I know I told you there's a trial period here; it's clear you will do fine, so I won't play bad cop with you anymore. I'm gonna work you harder than anyone, publicly praising but quietly critiquing you. I want to work with you to make you tougher—that is, if you're sure this is what you want. No bullshit, I don't have the time or energy to waste. This business is wicked. It spits out the weak, and I've seen it before. You're not the first talent Victor has warmed to. Keep your head on straight and keep it on tight."

I was sitting, nodding slowly and just listening to what he was saying. It took a minute to sink in. *Was Victor really involved here? How could I have not known this?* I looked at the floor, looked back up at him and said, "I can handle anything Chef, I assure you I am tougher than you think. I am sure this is what I want, I've never been surer of anything. I will dedicate myself to this at all costs. Just say what to do Chef and it will be done, and I will never let you down," I said, sitting up straight now and looking him dead in the eye.

"We will see, won't we Chef Cahill. We will see."

CHAPTER 17

TIME IS FLYING

The next two years were the fastest of my life, and moving equally as fast for Victor and Michael in New York. The boys from the Big Apple were as good as their word and their plan looked like it was coming together. Every time I picked up a newspaper I read about the Dexter House expansion. Victor was everywhere: not just in the food section, but in *Forbes*, *Fortune*, and even on the front page of the *New York Times*, which is huge. Chef Mike kept packing them in, and they had begun building their four new restaurants simultaneously. Victor was really putting it all on the line, and the restaurants were going to be the biggest and best New York had ever seen. I waited every day to hear something from them, but was surprisingly comfortable with what I was doing in Boston.

Chef was as good as his word as well and was working me to the bone. There were times when I worked in 45-day stretches with one day off and then I'd do it all over again. Working those kind of days, sometimes from nine in the morning until midnight, wasn't normal for the crew at The Moon Room but I was a lead-by-example kind of chef and wasn't about to let anyone work harder or longer than me. My dedication had won over the crew; they now respected me as a leader, and my age didn't matter anymore. Billy was slowly fading into the background, able to become a true Executive Chef as I was manning the kitchen with gusto. His focus was more on profit, menu development, marketing and growth while I spent my days manning the crew, expediting, creating new menu items and handling the overall internal operations. They were all behind me. Each and every one called me Chef, never Jack anymore, whether we were in the kitchen or at the bar. It filled me with great pride every time I heard it, too. It never got old to me. We were a great team and people were taking notice. We were getting more and more press by the day at The Moon Room, but the real story was back in New York.

I had learned from Billy to give back to the people who are good to you so Travis and Mario became my unofficial sous chefs. They executed my orders to a tee; hell, even Hack was behind me. It was a great feeling to have taken control. Some days I was even convinced they trusted me more than Billy.

I was always the type of Chef who liked to do it all himself. If I could, I would prep every single item that we sold, down to the garnish—but you can't, you need a team. If a chef tells you he does it all himself, he is lying through his teeth. Many are selfish and conceited, so they take the credit instead of sharing it. As I was learning how to do things from a chef's vantage point, this was becoming more and more clear. Chef William Steed was a great example of a chef who liked to give back to the people who do for him.

"Chef Jack, you got a second for me?" Billy asked, coming in from the dining room. I was just finishing peeling some roasted poblano peppers.

"Of course Chef," I said, taking off my gloves and heading out to the dining room with him.

He was ten paces ahead of me wearing his whites and he was walking towards a woman who was sitting down with a pad. She was an Asian woman wearing a blue suit with thick glasses and long black hair. She was very attractive and smiling as I approached. I was clean, but double-checked and dusted myself off before I got to the table.

"Chef Jackson Cahill, this is Anita Cheng. She's a food writer for the *Boston Globe*," Bill said, sliding into the booth. I stayed standing.

"Hello, it's nice to meet you," I said, extending my hand.

She stood up, "It's very nice to meet you Chef, William has said the nicest things about you." She shook my hand and smiled. She was very, very attractive.

"Well, the feeling is mutual; I'm privileged to be working with him."

"Funny," she said, biting the end of her pen, "he said the same thing about you." She slowly sat back down but never took her eyes off of me. "Won't you please sit?"

I slid in next to Billy, looked at him, and looked back at her. "So, what can I do for you?" I asked.

She paused for a second and then said "Well, I'm doing a story on Boston's hottest chefs so I came to see William. The Moon Room is up for best restaurant in next month's Best of Boston issue, as well as best nightlife, best service, and most creative menu. I mean, you guys are up for an awful lot this year, more than anyone, and you have the most coveted categories covered. Some might even say you guys are a lock," she said, winking at me and smiling. "I started talking to William and he insisted if I was going to do this that I would have to feature you and not him. He says um….that you're the real talent around here." She leaned in towards me, putting the pen back to her lips. "Is that true?"

"No, absolutely not, I mean, I am a part of what happens here but Chef is the heart and soul of this place. If anyone deserves the recognition it's him," I said with a look of total sincerity on my face, only to have it broken by their laughter.

"What's so funny?" I asked.

"I told ya," Chef said. "This boy is as sweet as strawberry pie, I told ya he'd say that." Chef was still smiling.

"You were right, he did say it," she said with her smile slightly fading, "And ah, he is pretty sweet."

"Jack, the truth is this award is big. You'll be well-known in this town as a result, and I can't accept the award. You do it all around here; you're the real heart and soul now. Times have changed and it's time you get recognized, time to pop that cherry of yours," he said, putting his arm around me.

"Ow....I like the sound of that," Anita said, still looking at me. "So Chef Jackson, what do you think, can I cover you? The story, that is."

I looked up at Chef. "You sure about this?" I asked him reluctantly.

"One hundred percent, you've earned this and then some. You're what this business is about, and it's time the world knew that," he said with a look of pride.

"OK, so it's settled. Chef Jackson Cahill, Boston's Hottest Chefs 2001," she said, starting to write.

"Jack, please call me Jack," I said, leaning back.

"Sure, I'll call you anything you want. And here is my number, you call me anytime you want." She stood up. "Bye Chef Jack, bye William." I couldn't help but watch her leave...., and Billy couldn't either.

"Wow! Chef, what the fuck, man? Why would you do this for me? This is huge, you deserve it. I mean I'm just a sous, is this even real?" Charles was walking over with a bottle of champagne.

"Oh, it's real Chef," *Pop!* Charles put the open bottle on the table.

"OK, now this concerns you!" Charles said, walking to the bar to get glasses. The restaurant was an awesome place to be in when it was closed, so much quieter and brighter. To me, it was the best office on Earth.

I smiled at Charles as he said, "If we're gonna officially be on the same level, can I at least tell people you're 25?" he said, now pouring.

"What do you mean?" My voice went up in pitch. I had an idea where this was going and I was eager.

Billy said, "Boston's Hottest Chefs, you little shit, you're 21 years old and you're one of Boston's Hottest Chefs, do you have any idea how huge this is for you?"

"Yes!" I exploded, "It's fucking *huge*! The guys are never gonna let me hear the end of this!" I said with a smile.

"Well, how about a toast," Billy said as we raised our glasses. "To Chef Jack Cahill, 21-year-old wunderkind, Boston's Hottest Chef, and . . ." he paused, "the new Executive Chef of The Moon Room," he said, holding his glass still.

"What?" I screamed. "What are you talking about Chef? What the hell are you talking about?"

"That's right Jack, it's your house now," Charles said.

"Chef, Billy, what are you saying, where are you going? What are you—"

Billy interrupted. "I got a call from Mike Roderick yesterday. I'm going to New York to open the second largest of the four new restaurants. It's huge, 300 seats, 2 levels, 2 kitchens, 120 cooks on staff, 4 sous chefs. They're laying out huge money, I mean wicked huge like never seen before money. The place is fucking pisser and Mike wants me to run it," he said, raising his glass slightly higher. "So, I guess there's reason for us all to celebrate today," he said, now clanking my glass.

"Wow, I mean wow Bill, that's huge." I had to clear my throat. "So Mike called you himself?" I asked. My mood changed; I'd just been named Boston's Hottest Chef, then got promoted, and shit I knew how much money Billy made a year and that was going to be amazing, big money, big job, big life and everything goes along with it. I'd live a life after sundown that most people dreamed of. It was the biggest thing that had ever happened to me, and I'd just started feeling settled. All my hard work was coming to fruition, and despite all the attention I was getting, and the perks that came along with it, I found myself at that moment thinking of Karen.

I thought of her often, but found creative ways to block her out. Moments like this brought more vivid images, and my thoughts were harder to shake. There were times when I felt I was doing all of this for her, like she was watching me and could see me at all times. The thought often motivated me. It didn't matter, though; I knew they were just thoughts and that she had been gone for years. Here and now was my focus, and here and now was pretty fucking cool.

Billy smiled from ear to ear. "Yes, he called me yesterday, God it was good to hear from the golden Mick, can't wait to get down there and take that city by storm. I'm leaving you the keys to the kingdom Jackie boy. You've earned them, and now they're yours and yours alone. Take good care of them," he said, raising his glass again. "Chefs, chefs for life," he said, slugging his champagne.

"Speaking of chefs, I've got to get back to work. We have a busy night ahead of us," I said, standing up. "Congratulations Chef, you deserve it," I said, turning and walking away.

"Chef Cahill," he shouted. I turned to see him and Charles looking at me. "So do you," he said, raising his glass one more time. I nodded and went back to work.

CHAPTER 18

BOSTON'S FINEST

I'd be lying if I said I didn't enjoy what was happening. The Chefs article would be printed in two days, the "Best of Boston" was right around the corner, and people were starting to know my name. It was pretty exciting. The nights that followed were late ones, the parties were all VIP, and the after-parties were even better. We did everything and anything we wanted—at least Billy and I did. Everyone knew him. Sometimes when he had one too many shots of whiskey, he talked about New York like he was a little scared, or at least nervous, though he never came right out and said it. Even Charles went out with us; he and Mike went way back, so I often wondered if he was a little jealous that he didn't get the call. He mentioned it every so often.

"I bet Victor's waiting on me for the big house—yeah that's it, when he gets closer to that four-dining-room spot he's building," Charles screamed over the music. It was Billy's last night so we were out partying hard. Charles asked, "What's he calling that one again?"

"Byzantine," I said quickly. "It means complex."

"Right, Byzantine," he said to Billy. "Four's better than one, eh Steed?" he said laughing.

"Well, it's two dining rooms dip shit, but yes, it's better," Billy said. "Do you know how much fucking money he put into those four restaurants? Forty million, that's crazy money!" Billy said, shaking his head. "And Byzantine is 20 of that million. He's hoping to get more than 1,000 people there a day; I mean, super Mike is gonna have his hands full packing that place everyday. I heard he was gonna man that one himself, guess he said he didn't trust anyone else with that much of the old man's money."

"Oh please," Charles screamed. The Hot House was packed and loud as hell, "Who does he think he is; we practically grew up in restaurants together. If he doesn't think he needs me down there then his ego is bigger then his big red beard," Charles said, grabbing his beer. He was a little buzzed up; he always got a little cranky when he was. "Anyway, this night is about you Bill. You're off to New York, at least let him know old Chucky would like a damn call every now and again."

"To Billy, good luck brother, make us proud!" I said, raising my glass. We all toasted as Charles sat back with a look of disgust on his face. No matter, he was right. This night was about Billy. Our leader was off to a bigger game, and it always made all of us proud when one of our own moved on for the right reasons. So many people washed out or gave up, switched careers, became teachers, got nine-to-fives at health care services or sold out to corporate gigs—anything but the real heart and soul of this industry, and that was trend-setting impendent restaurants that pushed hard to innovate and break the mold. Billy and I were certainly that type of chef, and The Moon Room was certainly that type of place.

We celebrated his good fortune the way all chefs do: lots of shots, drinks, smokes, girls, and laughter. We would miss him; we'd come a long way together. He was a great guy and we gave him a proper send-off.

Really buzzed up after a high-octane night, I headed home alone in a cab. I stumbled my way up the stairs, still laughing about it all in a great way. What a week. Turning on the light in my apartment, I realized that my place had come a long way too. It wasn't just a bed and boxes anymore—I had done it up nice; well, at least as nice as $700 a week can buy. I had a couch, televisions, and a stereo. My kitchen was the one room I didn't spend a lot on. I almost never cooked or ate at home; since I spent so much time at work I didn't even grocery shop. The only thing in my fridge was a filtered water pitcher, and bottles of ketchup, ranch dressing and hot sauce. My freezer held one whole ham, some mango chutney that had moved with me, and a couple of frozen pizzas. I turned on a little music and headed for my wine cabinet. I had a special bottle of Silver Oak 1997 that I had bought to celebrate the night Karen and I moved in together, but of course it hadn't happened. I turned up the music and cracked that baby open. I couldn't have been happier. Tomorrow the Globe would name me a top chef in Boston which I anticipated a big response from, and the next day was my first day as executive chef. I had an awesome city as my playground. There were always girls to pursue, though most of the time I had no connection. It was fun but felt empty. Although I was dedicated to my work, on occasion I wondered if I was missing something. Everything in life comes at a cost, and I had been missing everything back in Pleasant Valley: all of my friends' birthdays, weddings, holidays, you name it and I stopped attending it. I never left Boston; you'd be amazed how much you miss when the RSVP is always sent back with regrets. My family and friends were very supportive but I know they would have liked to see me have a little more balance. Life was one sided, all work all of the time which I loved, but when I had the rare moment to sit and think, all sorts of things would race through my head.

As the bottle got emptier and the city got quieter, Karen entered my mind as she often still did. I missed her very much and walked around the apartment that night wondering what it would look like had she been there with me. She would have hated some of the decorating I had done. She had very specific style and taste, and I always enjoyed watching her shop. Back in Hyde Park, we spent many nights lying awake talking about what our apartment would look like, where we would buy a home, where we would be in 10 years. Those were good dreams, dreams worth reminiscing about from time to time, though spending time wondering what could have been could often lead you to places you shouldn't go.

After pacing and pouring the last glass, I opened the box in the closet with our picture in it. There were some old CIA memories in there as well, some candid photos of us, and they made me smile. I also stumbled across our old phone list that we all got on graduation day, and sure enough, there was her number. Goddamn, wine just takes over sometimes. I knew it was late but I couldn't help but call her, so I did.

"Hi, you've reached Karen Macrillo," *fucking voice-mail*, "I can't come to the phone right now, so leave me a message and I'll get right back to ya! Bye now!" She sounded so perky and cute.

"Hey Karen, it's um, its Jack uh Cahill, Jack Cahill from Boston's," drunken idiot, I hadn't spoken for the last few hours I didn't even realize how slurry I sounded. "Um, anyway, just at our . . . my apartment in Boston and wanted to say hi. I'm duning, done. . . I'm doing very well here but missed, I mean thought of you tonight so I wanted to say hi . . . so . . . hello there, guess you're well, you sound well, on your message I mean so, good, that's good, everything's good, that's good to hear so, god . . . good night and see you around I suppose." I hung up, dazed.

I stood up, tipsy, and walked to the mirror. "Wow, you are a fucking idiot!" I said, very buzzed. I chugged back the last of the wine, fell onto the couch, and passed out.

CHAPTER 19

IN THE FLESH

I woke up the next day a little groggy after only getting four hours of sleep, but no matter—I had to get back to work. I showered, threw my knife kit over my shoulder, and hustled in.

As I was walking up, the boys were on the stoop smoking cigarettes. I stopped to catch up with them.

"Morning Chef," Hack said, "OK, I know I call you that all the time, but I can't believe little Elroy is officially our chef. If you weren't as good as you are, I wouldn't be able to say it with such a straight face," he said, slapping my face lightly.

"Thanks Hack, what's up guys? Anything going on?" I said, grabbing a smoke and sparking it up.

"No, usual, doesn't feel like anything's different, you're still the same ugly shit you were when you were sous,"

Mario joked. "Speaking of sous, you think of anyone yet to be yours? *Pick me!*" he said, coughing to disguise it. Everyone laughed.

"If I wasn't such an obvious choice that might be possible!" Travis joked.

"Oh please, Chef and I are like peanut butter and jelly, you little shits don't stand a chance!" Hack said, blowing out a cloud.

"That would be the fucking day!" Travis said, laughing so hard his coffee spilled all over Hack's shoes.

"Hey, watch it shit bag!" Hack scowled back.

"All right boys, all right, relax. I'll let everyone know soon enough, can we just get to work now?" I said, stomping out my cigarette.

"Dealing with these twits is a full-time job. Chopping shit will be a pleasure," Hack said, flicking his smoke and heading in. The boys headed to the kitchen as I went for the office. Deliveries were coming in, and Chef Kim was at her station and said good morning to me as I walked by. It felt great in there, like new air to breathe. I got to the office and started planning the night's specials.

Yukon Gold Blinis with Salmon Roe & Red Onion Crème Fraiche

Roasted Lamb Saddle, Zucchini Pancakes, Minted Onion Jam

Local Diver Scallops from Georges Bank, Sundried Tomato & Sweet Basil Risotto, California Balsamic

Charles walked in as I was writing. He was always very good about getting right back to work after a night out. He peeked at my scribbled-up menu.

"Looks good Chef," he said.

"Thanks Charles, what's going on?"

"Got some big players in the house, last minute change, the Red Sox are coming in tonight for dinner," he said, grabbing his calendar and writing something down.

"Which ones?" I asked.

"All of them, they were supposed to go to Smith and Wolinsky but guess they changed something. They called us so I'm reserving the PDR (private dining room) for them, should be very busy," he said, closing his calendar.

"It's all just tickets to me," I said. Tickets were what we called the dinner orders that came out of our kitchen printer from the servers. We were always so busy back there it really was all the same. I made sure everything was perfect no matter who was there.

"I know it, but let's pay extra attention to these guys. This is their first team visit with us so we need a homerun — no pun intended."

"You can count on it man," I said, not fazed by the celebrity. We had seen plenty come through the doors, from Will Smith to Robin Williams to Meryl Streep and more; we had seen our share there. Charles always got a little star struck but I just kept business as usual. Truthfully, my head hurt a little and I was embarrassed that I had called Karen, a rookie mistake I assured myself would never happen again.

The Sox party was huge. When a pro team comes in for a celebration they spend big. Ball players are big guys so they eat big, and they have the money so they drink even bigger. This was the 2001 kickoff party, between preseason and the start of the regular season, so it was cause for big celebration. Having celebrities in the building always made other people much more excited, so they drank a little more and spent a little more, as a result. This recipe worked out very well for me; because of all the excitement, we broke our personal high sales record that night. Not bad for my first night. In addition to the sales, our service was flawless—a record night with no long tickets and no re-fires, absolutely amazing. I couldn't have been happier with the crew. After a great party, the Red Sox coach Jimmy Williams asked me to come out and meet the team. It was cool to be hanging out with legends like Jason Varitek and Nomar Garciaparra. I shook their hands, wished them well for the season, and they assured me they'd be back many times over. It was such a great night that after 15 long hours, I couldn't believe it was already 1am. I got changed, washed up and shut the lights off in the kitchen for the day before deciding to do something I almost never did: I sat at our bar and had a drink. I always wanted to set a good example; I didn't like the cooks and servers who prepare the meals to then sit there in the restaurant and drink after their shift so I never did either. It always cheapened the experience in my eyes, though Charles never enforced it, I did all I could do to discourage it.

"Cold beer Chef?" Scottie the bartender asked as I leaned up against the bar.

"No, how about a glass of Louis tonight Scottie," I said, pulling up a chair.

"That good of a night, huh Chef?" he said, grabbing a snifter glass. We sold Louis for $150 a glass.

"Yeah Scottie, certainly felt that way," I said, putting my elbows on the bar and getting comfortable. I tried not to make eye contact with anyone as they were all looking in my direction. Most knew who I was and the scene was still alive, even for the late hour. As I was getting comfortable a newspaper flew over my shoulder and landed right in front of me.

"A lot less missed opportunities these days, I see." I couldn't believe my eyes, it was Victor Payne, just in from the cold wearing a full-length black trench coat, a white cashmere scarf, and checking his Rolex. "Scottie, leave the bottle, I've got some time to kill."

"Victor," I said, exasperated.

"In the flesh kiddo, I told ya I'd come looking for you one day. I got to tell ya Jack, I hate the ride up here, but I'd probably hate it a lot more if I didn't have my friend Dom Perignon to keep me company. Only problem is he doesn't look as good as her," he said, pointing to a group of girls, "or her . . . or her . . . hello ladies. Scott, let's get a couple more stools over here, we have some celebrating to do!" The girls were waving and smiling.

"What are you doing here?" I asked in a state of pure awe. I couldn't believe he was here.

"Well," he was taking off his coat and sitting down, "oh, cheers by the way," he said routinely, toasting to start his conversation and sipping his Louis. "Ahhhh….Goddamn that's good Jack, you have good taste kid. I like that my boys have good taste; it shows my eye still works. Turn to the food section," he said, pointing at the newspaper he'd thrown. Right there on the cover of the Boston Globe's food section I stood—my photo, my biography, the headline "Boston's Hottest Chefs"—and I was number one. I was overwhelmed.

"I didn't realize they were rating us," I said slowly. I could feel a tear in my eye. I made sure to wipe it quickly and acted nonchalant. I was in disbelief.

"Everything is rated, young man. Just when you think it's not a competition is the minute you get soft, just then, BAM," he said, slapping the bar top, "somebody else is number one, they gotcha, and it's an awful decay from there." He finished his glass, and I had still barely sipped mine. "I like this Louis, but I have something here that will blow your mind. But first, go get those ladies and come sit at my table. Scott, have the Louis sent over and tell Charles to get my Chateau d' Yquem—it's from 1784 Jackie, HA! This is going to be a good night!"

The restaurant was now closed but Victor insisted that some customers stay. He always liked to feel like he was in the place to be. Naturally, the four girls came to sit with us and he kept pouring and pouring, great bottle after great bottle. I was shocked to learn a few of them cost up to $5,000 a bottle. I had no idea that wine could cost so much! He was in his own league, not just with money but with personality; he was larger than life.

As he poured a bottle of Screaming Eagle Cabernet next he asked, "So Jack, what's been going on around here." This was very reminiscent of the night we had in New York, only I was sitting in Mike's seat and wow, that thought gave me chills.

"Business as usual Victor," I said calmly.

"HA! You all say that, but you know there's a lot of dull knives out there, trust me, I've had them. But sometimes there are guys like Mike out there, guys who know their trade. As someone who graduated with a business degree from Yale, and a master's from Columbia, I can tell you the world thought I was insane to get into the restaurant business. But I know something they don't know Jack . . ." He paused to sip from his $4,000 bottle of Cabernet.

"What is that, Victor?" I did the same.

"Talent my boy! It sounds so simple, but it's *talent* that makes this world go 'round, *talent* that make a film into a blockbuster, *talent* that sells out stadiums just to hear them sing, *talent* that wins Super Bowls, *talent* my boy, no matter what field you're in, it's *talent*. Ha ha! You get it? I spent $150,000 on education to learn I didn't need to know anything except how to find the ones who do, and coach them properly! It's so simple yet few people figure it out!" he said as one of the girls was pulling at his necktie.

"I have talents too Victor," she said, leaning in closer.

"Oh I have no doubt that you do, and no doubt you're as eager to show them as I am to see them!" he said, smiling at her. "But first sweetheart, Jack and I have some business to discuss. Then we'll all go back to my suite and we can have a little talent show of our own. What do you say to that?" he said, quickly licking his lips.

"Oh, I like it Victor," she said, turning back to her girlfriend and whispering something in her ear. Her eyes and mouth both opened wide and she slapped Victor's arm from across the table. The music was loud and the vibe was perfect.

"You're a bad boy, where did you come from!" her friend said as they grabbed at each other playfully. He winked at her and turned back my way.

"Good stuff, very good stuff. Life is fun but it's also very distracting, you always have to get the job done before it's time to play! You tell me business as usual, well, let me see for myself." He pointed at Scottie who came over immediately with a folder. "Costs down 13%, overall sales up 25%, food sales up 40%, record breaking sales tonight, Boston's Best Chef, and my sources tell me you are about to win Best Restaurant in Boston by the *Globe* in 2 weeks. Forget all the other awards, they're chicken shit compared to that. That's the only one that matters. This record is incredible," he said a little more seriously as he closed the file.

"We have a good team here Victor, and Billy—"

"HA!" Victor burst out, "Billy, he's good I'll give him that, but he's no you. The stats don't lie, kid! These numbers reflect our restaurant since you walked through the door. Billy had three years, here are his stats: sales flat, costs up 3%, no awards in the last two years, missing inventory, sloppy receiving, things I know you saw, what else is there to say! He did better than most but I made sure he didn't get that award. It's your name that needs to be in the headlines, kid!"

"So you arranged for his transfer to get me this award?" I asked, listening closely.

"Yes, but he's not going to be running the show down there, your old sous chef Lance Issacs will be. Billy will be sous. They'll be running Current, on the Upper West Side. I have three others opening: Trist in Soho, Maison in Midtown, and our biggest of all will be Byzantine. Mike will be running them all. But make no mistake about it Jack, the transfer didn't get you the award, your incredible talent did, something this world is lacking." He grabbed the bottle and filled his glass.

"So what brings you here tonight?" I asked.

"Jack Jack Jack, you don't miss an opportunity any more do ya! You have come a long way. Your dedication to your trade is unparalleled. You have set this restaurant on a good course. The holes in the ship have been plugged. It will take much time before the reputation you have built fades away; Travis and Charles can keep us going strong now. It is time to put you to the ultimate test to see how much you can handle before you break!"

"I think I'm following Victor, but I'm not sure I'm ready for what you are asking me," I said calmly.

"Scottie! Bring us a couple of shots of my 60-year-old Maccallen. My trip was worth it, I just found the guy I was looking for! Ladies, feast your eyes on New York City's newest and biggest chef! Twenty-one years old and in charge of the biggest restaurant in the US! Ha! Hot damn I knew it all along!" he said, getting into that Victor Payne late night stride.

"Victor, I just told you I don't think I'm ready for it," I repeated.

"That's how I know you *are,* my boy. Your record speaks for itself. I spoke to Charles Hayes today, and he said when he told you the Sox were coming in you said, 'it's all just tickets to me and you make it great no matter who it's for.' That's the kind of guy I need, one who's not fazed by the celebrity, one who only wants to kick ass with his troops, clean up, and get right back to it tomorrow. Billy told me you did 45 days in a row without a day off or a single complaint—my kind of chef, not just talented but dedicated! I've eaten at the best restaurants in the world, I've searched high and low, and there are guys out there like you, not many, but they are there and hard to find. I've already found you, so it's time to give you what you deserve. Young or not, you're the right guy for the job my boy, I just know it."

"Well, I don't know what to say, I'm honored that you think this of me Victor, I truly am. If you feel this strongly about it, then count me in," I said as Scottie was delivering the shots.

"You are something! What about money, relocation expenses, benefits, you're not even gonna ask!" he said, raising his glass as a little spilled down his hand.

"I don't have to; besides, we've got a talent show to get to." I clinked his glass and we did our shot.

He looked at me, half smiled, then burst out, "HA! Damn right we do! You start in five days, you're officially done here. Get your life in order and I'll email you your new address! Welcome to the big game Jack, I can't wait to see what you do next!"

"Victor, come on, we're dying to see your limo," the girls said, standing up and pulling him by his tie.

"It's a Rolls Royce ladies," he said as he winked at me and followed them out. I smiled and even laughed out loud a little; what the hell had just happened to me? I stood up and looked around The Moon Room, a place that had been awfully good me, a place I would never forget. As I slid on my coat I heard Scottie say, "Boy that Victor is something, huh Chef?"

"Yeah Scottie, I'd say he is." I was stunned.

"See you tomorrow, huh Chef?"

"Yeah, Scottie, see you tomorrow," I said softly. I walked to the door, took one last look, and headed out. The Rolls was parked out front and the door was open, I could hear girls laughing and screaming with loud music coming from inside. I watched Victor grab the door, smile at me deviously for a second and slam it closed. For Victor, business was over and the party had just begun.

CHAPTER 20

THERE SHE WAS

In a lot of ways, Victor Payne was like a tornado: he swept into town unexpectedly, you're defenseless to his powers, he turned your world upside down, and just like that, he was gone. I didn't get home until about 2:30am and I was undoubtedly drunk, but even more importantly I was flying high on life. I was wiped, burning the candle at both ends and now I had to get ready to head back to New York. This was insane, just when things were getting settled, just when my crew was in line, just when I was comfortable it was time for another shake up. I was getting use to it, things changed quickly with Victor; you had to learn how to react at the drop of a hat, that was just the way he was.

I headed to the restaurant around 10am, still a little tipsy, but nothing some coffee and a pair of sunglasses couldn't take care of. As I walked in Charles was there.

"Goddamn you, I mean really, Jack? How is that possible? I've been working here for five years. I've known Victor for ten, Mike for fifteen. How do you get this after just two years? He looked sincerely worked up.

"Relax Charles, I didn't do anything."

"Oh please, I should have known something was up when he called yesterday. 'The next Michael Roderick' I see, well all hail the almighty Jack Cahill. Good luck back in New York, hope you choke on it." He walked away pissed and threw his clipboard against the ice machine.

"What an asshole," I said to myself, heading into the kitchen to say my goodbyes.

"There he is ladies and gentlemen! Jack Cahill, must be bored with walking on water to come see us!" Mario said humorously.

"Guess so boys," I smiled. They all stopped what they were doing and came over to say goodbye.

"You know, most chefs that only last a day don't get life-altering promotions!" Travis said, shaking my hand. "Congratulations Chef, you deserve it." He pulled me in for a hug.

"Thanks Travis, I can't thank you guys enough for everything these past few years. It's been amazing, and you are the best of the best as far as I'm concerned. I'm proud to say I worked with you."

"I'm proud to say I no longer do!" Hack said playfully, laughing while shaking my hand "Now get over here and give me a hug you little shit."

"Hack I would, but you're the only guy who's *this* dirty by 10am!" Everyone laughed, but he was already filthy somehow.

"Tough shit!" He grabbed me and picked me up. "We'll miss ya Elroy!"

"Same to you guys. I'll be back for pre-meal tonight. I wish we could have one more night but it's Victors order, I have to be in New York in 4 days. I literally have to move tomorrow."

"We know, Charles told us . . .and *woooooo*, he had smoke coming out of his ears boy, I tell ya what!" Mario said.

"I know; we had a 'pleasant' conversation about it this morning," I said with sarcasm.

"I bet. Now get out of here buddy, we'll see you later! All right boys back to work," Travis said, getting back to it himself.

"Yes Chef," I heard Mario say with a hint of sarcasm in his voice. I guess the order had already come down: Travis was in charge and I was on my way back to New York.

When I arrived in Cambridge to pack later that day, I saw a truck parked out front and four guys waiting on my stoop.

"You Jack Cahill?" he asked, big guy, really big.

"That's me, can I help you?"

"Yeah, we're here to move you, can you let us in? Should only take us an hour or so." he said, checking his pager.

I gave him a confused look as he flipped a page on the clipboard. "We got a call from a Victor Payne's office, said be here at noon, we'll have to get this stuff to New York by morning. He said don't worry about it, check your email, he'll send a car for you tomorrow. Can we get to it now?" he said, flipping the page back.

"Yeah sure," I said, mildly exasperated but not totally surprised knowing Victor. As I reached for my keys, the mover handed me a note:

"Jack, don't worry, the movers they will take care of everything. I have arranged for you to stay at the Four Seasons tonight; just go to the desk and they'll have an envelope with some spending cash for you. Tomorrow a car will pick you up and take you to your new apartment in New York City. It's in the financial district right by Battery Park, you'll love it—quintessential New York living, Jack. Safe travels, enjoy your last night in the minors, see you in 4 days."

Victor

P.S. The blonde won the talent contest last night!

New York, right where I knew I belonged. I raced upstairs and threw a few things in my backpack to get me through the night, then hopped a taxi to the restaurant to say goodbye to everyone at pre-meal. Once again, Charles was at the door as I walked in.

"Got a minute?" he asked. He was in full suit; he was actually a very professional person when he wasn't being a total dick.

"Yeah what's up?" I asked.

"Sorry about before man, just blowing off some steam. I mean, I'm definitely more qualified than you but I shouldn't have acted up. Still friends I hope?" He stuck out his hand.

"Fuck you," I said and I walked away shaking my head. It felt great too; he was always a little arrogant, one trait I couldn't stand. I headed for the kitchen, where I was met with some tears. Servers and bartenders alike were sad to see me go. I told them all I would miss them and be back, although inside I felt I never would be.

"Who am I gonna gaze at all night now . . . Hack?" Jason said with a tear in his eye.

"You'll be fine buddy, just—wait, you were gazing at me?" I asked, half kidding.

"Yes! And now you're gone and this place will never be the same, I've been here since the beginning and now we suck again!" He was literally crying.

"There there Jay, you'll be OK. Travis is great, and besides, he's sort of cute," I said, trying to console him.

"I guess," he said, wiping his tears and taking a deep breath.

"Now take care buddy," I said to him as I gave him one more hug.

"I'll try Chef. We'll miss you though, seriously," he said one more time.

"Me too Jason, good luck my friend." Our hug ended and I turned to head out.

I was leaving now, officially, my last days here. I was still months from even being 22 years old and I was already heading for the big time. Determined and focused, I paced towards the door when I heard, "Chef, Chef!" It was Scottie running towards me.

"Uh, yeah Scottie, what's up?" I asked him with one foot already out the door.

"Another panting fan of yours at the bar, want me to tell her you left or do you want one last hurrah?" he asked. There was always some girl asking about Billy or me; there were always one or two at the bar looking to meet us. I thought about it for a second but was pretty tired, and anxious to get going.

"Ah, let her know I've left for the day. I'm still wiped from last night if you know what I mean," I said kidding around.

"You got it Chef, take care of yourself," Scottie said, shaking my hand. He was a nice guy, a little older, and had been in this business a long time. "You too Scottie," I nodded as he walked away.

Heading to the door I figured it would at least be worth a look, so I glanced at the bar as I kept walking. I saw a girl, curly brown hair, reading *The Globe* and drinking a glass of white wine. My heart literally sank into my stomach when I realized it was Karen! Her head was turned and I could barely see her face, but it was definitely her. She looked absolutely beautiful, astonishingly so. *Dear God, what the hell is going on here? Why today, why now?* I had no choice but to go see her, but my hands were shaky and sweaty and I was as nervous as I had ever been. I took a deep breath and started walking in her direction, and as I did she caught me out of the corner of her eye.

"Of all the things your stumbly little voice could have told me the other night and you didn't mention this!" she said, slapping the paper with the back of her hand.

"Well I thought 'uh . . . uh . . . uh' was more appropriate," I said, just one step away. All of the sudden I felt looser just being in her presence, almost like no time had passed at all.

"How are you?" she said, smiling and giving me the biggest hug she ever had. She smelled so good and so familiar.

"I'm well, how are you? Where are you? You look great!" I said, grinning like a school boy.

"So do you! I mean really great, and what the hell is this, I leave you alone for a couple of years and you decide to take over the city!" she said completely smiling. Her smile was so intoxicating and I felt like even though she smiled often, that one was special, just for me. "OK, to answer your questions, I'm well thank you very much, where am I, Boston Massachusetts, and thank you, I feel great!" she said totally laughing and flirting. I couldn't help but laugh too—really, really laugh in a way I had almost forgotten that I could.

"Wow, I can't believe you're here," I said, still half hugging her.

"I can't believe you called! I called you back, left you two messages, and when I didn't hear back, I thought I would just come here to see you! Did you plan for this to happen, I know you can be a little psychic sometimes!"

"How do you mean planned?" I said, raising one eyebrow.

"I mean, here is today's paper and you just got named Boston's Hottest Chef. Now, I always thought you were pretty hot but for the whole city to think so? And then you called and I'm here — I think you're just showing off!" she said, slapping my stomach and laughing. She was always very slappy and playful with me.

"I didn't, and I would say I'm sorry for the drunken call the other night, but you're here, so I'm sort of not sorry anymore," I said in disbelief that she was actually standing there, right in front of me.

"I'm not either," she said in a little more serious tone. She hesitated for a second just to look at me, then she said, gazing into my eyes, "So super chef . . . buy a girl a drink?" My heart almost stopped with her presence but I didn't want her to know that.

"I'd love to, but not here. I know a place you'll love—come on, I'll take you there."

"I'd love to, but don't you want to show me your place?" she said, still gazing at me.

"This isn't my place anymore," I said.

"What do you mean?" she said slowly.

"Come on, it's a long story but mainly I want to hear about you!" I said sincerely.

We left The Moon Room for the last time; it was ironic that it was with the person I went there for in the first place. We stopped by the Four Seasons to drop off Karen's car and pick up Victor's envelope, which held $5,000 and a note that said "Signing bonus, have fun!" He was incredible.

With the money Victor left me I took Karen to Clio, one of Boston's best restaurants. As we ate I explained everything, from my heartbreak to my anger, from Billy to Victor. I was open about it all. She was the one person I could talk to calmly. She made my heartbeat still and kept my hands from shaking—my hands often shook, but not when we were together. It felt amazing to be with her there, and we were treated like royalty at Clio, thanks to the article. It was truly a meal to remember. Clio was the hottest restaurant at the time, and Ken Oringer was Boston's most famous and well-respected chef.

"Chef Cahill, Chef Oringer would like to say congratulations with this, his favorite bottle in the house." It was a 1982 Rothschild, a very, *very* good bottle of wine.

"He is too kind. Please let him know I am appreciative, as well as a fan of his." I said coolly. Being with Karen really made me feel like myself, and on top of the world.

"So Jack, is this what you have gotten used to without me around?" she asked very sweetly, curling up next to me.

"Actually, quite the opposite. I've gotten very used to solitude," I said.

"What do you mean solitude, you have everything! You're on your way, I mean really on your way! You're going to New York City to open a Victor Payne restaurant. I mean, holy shit Jack, this is what you told me years ago, your name in lights. I can't imagine a better ending to your climb. This is the top. I hope it feels good, better than—" she paused, fidgeting a little with her wine.

"Better than what, Karen?" I asked, grabbing her hand. She looked up at me with those blue eyes, and a look of disappointment took her over.

"…better than nothing Jack. I don't even have a job. That's not why I'm here by the way, I couldn't care less about Byzantine or The Moon Room, about Boston, the award, Victor, all of it. I just wish sometimes . . . well, I guess I wish life hadn't intervened the way it did," she said, slowly rubbing her finger on my hand. Those words couldn't have hit any closer to home.

"Well it may seem that way, but work has become my life. I've sort of been reprogrammed over the last couple of years. Yes, I'm around people all day but most of the time I'm alone with my thoughts. I've sat on my balcony more times than you would believe just staring out into the city. I don't go home to see my family, I don't make time for friends, I don't date. I live to be a chef and that's all I have," I said as the server cleared our plates. I took another sip of wine as she gazed at me from across the table.

"Only you," she said, tilting her head and staring directly into my eyes.

"Only me what?" I asked, smiling.

"Only you could have all this and say you have nothing," she said, reaching for my hand.

"Well," I said, looking at her fingers rubbing mine, "I do have my balcony," I said sarcastically, trying to add levity to the mood.

"You mean at our place . . . the place we picked?" she said, smiling again.

"Yes, it's empty but I still have the keys. Will you come with me to our place?" I asked as she touched my wrist and moved her hand back down to my fingertips. "I don't want to do anything but be near you, nothing but hear your voice."

"Yes Jack, I would love to," she said with a full smile on her face. We were so anxious we asked for the bill and left before dessert came.

"Chef Oringer sends his regards," she server said as we were walking out.

"And we send our compliments. Please give him our most sincere thanks," I said with my arm around Karen.

"You've gotten good at this," she said as we walked out. We looked at each other, smiled wholeheartedly, and left.

We grabbed a taxi back to our place. Karen had not been there since we chose it a couple of years before. She was leaning back in the cab's seat totally struck by me, and I in return was in total awe that someone so beautiful could be looking at me that way. I was in a state of shock. We had stopped to buy a couple of fine bottles thanks to Victor's cash: a 1990 Far Niente Chardonnay and a bottle of Krug Rose champagne. We got back to my—well, our place around 10pm.

"I remember coming here like it was yesterday," she said as she got out of the cab. She was looking the building up and down.

"It's come and gone quickly," I said.

"I'm sorry that it did," she said, grabbing my hand.

"As am I. Let's go relax and not worry too much about it," I said as I was holding $1200 in wine in my hands. I guess Victor was rubbing off on me. I took her out on the balcony, which she hadn't noticed when we came here the first time together.

"You're right, it's totally ratty!" she said, bursting into laughter.

"I told ya!" The few chairs that were up there were busted apart with holes in them. "Sorry!"

"Oh please, it's just nice to here," she said sitting down.

"Baby, what happened, where have you been working? Please tell me I didn't interfere with you career."

"Ha ha . . . oh no Jack, you're powerful but not that powerful. Life hasn't been easy these last few years. In school I was sure of myself, at least in the beginning I was, but the longer I was there the harder it was for me. In the real world, I only went so far. You were right Jack, I was wrong to leave you, all wrong. I was mad about Molly, I truly was, however there's another reason I didn't come here with you. I haven't been working. I took a job back home that was so far beneath me it made me cry night after night. Cooking fish on a fry station with a CIA degree, no offense, but really? I busted my butt for them, 70 hours a week, and they didn't even pay me overtime. Anytime I questioned it, they just said there's the door, but my pride prevented me from quitting, I didn't want to be a failure, not for myself, not for you, not for anyone, but eventually it was too much for too little. They paid me next to nothing, literally a step above minimum wage. Everyone thinks the CIA is some magical doorway to the end of the rainbow—how little we knew, I guess. What was it you always said to me? 'Our education will begin the minute we walk out the door.' I laughed at those words then, at least inside I did. You were so young; I didn't think you could be right, but you were. After failing to find work that suited me, I headed back this way. I wanted a job here in Boston but couldn't find one either. I knew where you were, but I couldn't come see you with no job or promise and you doing *sooooo* well. A lot kept me from coming to see you," she said with utmost honesty.

I leaned forward in suspense and grabbed her hand tighter. "Look at me," I said, "what could possibly have kept you from coming here?" I was dumbfounded.

"Pride," she said quietly as she looked up at me. "I don't know, Jack; fear, insecurity, shame, I don't fucking know!" she screamed before calming down, "but I'm here now, and I know I feel closer to you than I have ever felt to anyone before."

"Neither have I!" I said, breathing a little heavier then usual. "I don't care about any of this, I see how clearly I care about you, how much I care about this night, us, I think, I . . . I think, I . . ."

"Yes Jack, what do you think?" She was gently touching my face, and I wanted so badly to tell her I loved her. Everything was racing through my mind; I wanted to scream it from the rooftop! But I didn't, I knew she wanted to hear it again but I couldn't say it, no matter how much it was killing me to keep it inside. I had to keep it in check. Life was going so well and this was a potential obstacle. I loved her more than anything but had to proceed with caution.

"I think we should change the subject." I took her hand off my face slowly. "I mean, here you are after all this time, who cares about it all. I have missed us so much, and I want to hear about the good. Certainly there's good. And I'd love to hear more about the fry station," I said, grinning and lighting up a smoke.

"Are you mocking me?" she said with a cute smile.

Starting to laugh I said, "Was it all catfish or were you doing crawfish and shrimp too?"

"Shut up!" she said, slapping my arm and easing some of the tension. I burst out laughing as we both sat back and looked at the city. "There may have been a few shrimp." We both died laughing and stared off into the city. "We can't all be Jack Cahill," she said, reaching out for my hand.

As she did I leaned into her, "I'm really glad you're here right now." She smiled with that same smile I remembered from a much simpler time.

"Me too. Thanks for this, I needed it, and I'm just gonna do this," she said as she leaned in closely, so close I could smell her very familiar breath. I loved it so much. She stayed close for just a minute, put her hand on the back of my head, pulled me in closer, and kissed me. How I had longed for that kiss; memories came flashing back to me, our whole history flashed before my eyes. I even saw the pictures I had always wished to see, pictures of our future. It was a very long, very passionate kiss that made some-thing inside of me awaken that had been asleep for some time. I wanted it to last forever, for that moment never to end. As blown away as I felt, I was also scared out of my mind that she was there. I loved her more than life itself, but what now?

After the most incredible kiss of my life we hailed a cab back to the Four Seasons—ironically the place Karen was hoping to work when we first came to Boston. We got there very late, but the night never ended. We drank more wine, laughed harder than either of us had ever laughed, and made love like it was the first time. It was amazing. It made me feel like a different person, whole and complete. She was my other half, and now she was back. I'd tried so hard to forget; there had been days when I had been able to block it out, to pretend I was strong enough to go on without her, powerful enough to make it alone, but I hadn't ever been sure that was true. I loved her and felt like I needed her and wanted her around me always. She was the one person who made me feel this way, the person I would never wrong or hurt. It was so good to feel this way again, and this time I hoped that feeling would last forever.

CHAPTER 21

BECOME WHO YOU WERE MADE TO BE

Waking up the next day was like waking up to a dream. The suite was amazing. We woke up to a knock on the door, "Good morning Mr. Cahill, your breakfast has arrived." I put on my plush white robe while Karen stayed in bed, wrapping herself in the sheets. As I opened the door, six servers swooped in with cart after cart of amazing breakfast items: fresh fruits, an assortment of pastries, and a chef to make us omelets and crepes to order. We sipped freshly brewed espresso and drank orange juice that was juiced right there in front of us, it was like nothing I had ever seen before, we felt like royalty. Karen and I indulged in everything, overlooking Boston, eating and talking about our future. After all, I was headed to New York and Karen was back. I was already reaping the benefits of my career, and now with her here I felt unstoppable.

"So, Victor should be sending us a car in a couple of hours. I can't wait to see our new place in New York, Karen. Finally we can have all we ever talked about! I am so happy that you're here for this, we'll get you a job in no time, especially with my new contact list —that is, if you think you want one. If not, Byzantine will keep us both plenty comfortable and with my . . ." I saw her shying away; she looked a little uncomfortable. "Did I say something wrong baby?" I asked, consoling her.

"No, of course not, you're absolutely wonderful."

"Then what is it?"

"Jack, I can't go with you, this is crazy," she said shyly. "I just came to see you last night. Yes, I was hoping we would be here today, but I didn't expect any of this. I mean New York over night, this is just crazy!" I was completely dumbfounded. "Let me rephrase," she said gently. "I did expect this, in fact, it's all I have thought about since we were last together, but you're off to a new city to become the chef of what promises to be the best restaurant in New York. You are leaving a city that just named you the best here as well, and I have nothing. I can't be responsible for slowing you down, not now, not when you're moving this fast."

"Karen, what the hell are you talking about? I've waited forever for you to return, I'm not going to let you go! No, I won't even let the thought enter my mind," I said, grasping at her as she grasped back.

"I've waited forever too Jack, and now I feel like I've waited for too long. Last night was beyond what I thought it could be. You put me right back where we left off. You are an amazing person, very gifted and talented, and above all you are very loving. I love you Jack, I know you love me too, but this isn't right of me to do. I can't just dive into this, not now at least, not this quickly," she said, holding back her tears.

"What are you talking about? This is what we have always talked about, all of our dreams are coming true!"

"No Jack, all of *your* dreams are coming true. You are doing everything you ever said you would. You are living your destiny, making your life exactly what you said you would all those years ago. *I'm not you, OK?* I'm *not*! I've done *nothing*! And I won't slow you down, I can't, you've done so much without me, I just can't insert myself into your new world, at least not now." A tear ran down her face.

"Karen, I'm not letting you go," I said, letting a tear run down my face.

"You have to, because I'm letting you go."

"No, Karen *I love you*! Please don't do this to me, not now!"

"I can't, Jack. I love you so much, but I can't. Go be the man I know you are. I love you and will be there with you. I hope one day when the time is right we can be together and I hope that day is soon," she said, getting up from her chair. "I hope for that more than anything, but now is all wrong, it just is Jack whether you want to admit it or not. This would be totally selfish of me to just cling to you right here and right now and I won't do that. I won't do that for my own reasons but even more importantly I wouldn't do that to you. I didn't know what to expect when I came to see you last night, but I certainly didn't expect to turn my life upside down. We could take things slow, but if your asking me to just jump into the deep end and move with you to New York then the answer is no baby, I just can't do that."

"Karen, trying to forget us these last few years has been the hardest thing I've ever had to do. I've waited for this moment for so long, I've pictured what I would say and what I would do a thousand times over in my head. I used that as fuel to make me stronger, it gave me direction when I needed it most. I thought for sure if and when you returned that this time would be different, but it's not. You don't know what you want Karen, you haven't in a long time. Well I do, and I always have, I want you but if you don't feel the same way then just get the hell out of here and stop wasting my time," I said, drying my tears. I firmed up quickly. My heart was breaking, but I wasn't about to show it. I folded my hands and looked away.

"No Jack, you have this all wrong," she said as more tears ran down her face.

Still looking away, I said definitely, "You came here as I have life under control, you made me fall in love again, and you're just willing to walk away again?" My eyes were totally dry now.

"No, Jack, that's not at all what I am trying to do. This night meant everything to me, you mean everything to me!" she said, intensifying her sadness.

"Well, that's exactly what the fuck you've done!" I shouted, flipping over the breakfast table. She stood up abruptly and backed up to the wall. I calmed a little and said, "You need to go, Karen. I've been made a fool of for the last time."

"Jackson Cahill, you have this all wrong!" she said, stepping to the door. "I'm sorry, so sorry for everything. I love you and will always love you. If our futures are meant to be together like I feel they are, then they will be," she said, grabbing her coat.

"Just go Karen," I said, looking away. I could not believe what I was hearing.

"I love you," she said as she walked out the door. The sound of it closing behind her was deafening. I felt like a fool. I recognized that feeling; it was distant but all too familiar. I stood strongly for a minute, hoping, I guess, that she would come back, but when she didn't my knees buckled and I sat down. I didn't cry any longer though. I felt completely empty inside, hollow actually, like a man with no heart. The phone rang.

"Yes Mr. Cahill, this is the front desk. Your car is here to take you to New York."

"Thank you, I'll be right down," I whispered in a smoky voice. I had nothing so I had nothing to pack. I grabbed my shoulder bag and headed out.

My time in Boston had come full circle; it was intended to be a life built for Karen and me, and it just wasn't. It was a town in where I was alone, despite all the action, the high life, the parties and the recognition. Karen made me feel complete, and I had always hoped it was to be us, but I was finished with putting my life on hold. I was so fucking mad I didn't know how to react, but I had much more going for me. I felt hurt and permanently scarred. My goal was never to look back — and now, once and for all, I knew I wouldn't.

Stepping out front I saw a black Lincoln. The driver opened the door and inside was a bottle of Louis Roederer

Cristal, one of the world's best champagnes, with a note: *"Next stop, destiny," - Victor.* I couldn't even open the bottle; I just lay down and went to sleep.

CHAPTER 22

BYZANTINE

If waking up with Karen had been like waking up to a dream, then waking up in New York was like waking up from that dream. I was in my reality. I felt hard as nails, and my only goal was to put her behind me immediately and focus on all that I had. I checked into my amazing new apartment; Victor hadn't been kidding. Beautiful park views, two bedrooms, high ceilings, amazing lighting, hardwood floors, and all of my furniture had been delivered along with a few new additions thanks to Victor. Everything had been unpacked and set up for me. As I turned the corner, I was greeted by a very unexpected visitor.

"I would give you the whole 'you do as I say when I say' speech, but something tells me you don't need it anymore." It was Michael Roderick, my Chef, my mentor, my idol. I was blown away that he was there.

"Quite a welcome wagon," I said, stepping towards him for a handshake.

"Good to see you Jack. My student is now ready to be the teacher," he said, looking me dead in the eye as he always did.

"I am, Chef, I am ready, willing and 100% focused on making this work," I said still shaking his hand. "And I am honored that you have selected me."

"Well, I will admit it was a hard choice. Victor came to see you on our behalf. He needed to know we were right. He says we are . . . what do you think?" Mike was all business, as always.

"I know you are Chef," I said, attempting to keep my composure.

"Good. I believe we are, Victor believes we are, and Charles believes we are." I was shocked to hear that. "However, William Steed has his reservations. Perhaps he is envious of your new position, but he feels as though you're not quite ready for the spotlight. Is there any truth to what he says?"

Without hesitation I said, "Absolutely not Chef, and I'm surprised to hear he said that. I handled our kitchen with great dignity, never succumbing to any of the temptations around me. With all due respect to Chef Steed, I wish I could say the same about him. I am ready for what lies ahead Chef, so ready I would like to drop my bag and get immediately to work."

"I'm glad to hear you say that. This restaurant is already New York's most talked about, bigger than Daniel, bigger than Jean Georges, bigger than Nobu. I am so far the face of it all, but the media wants to know who will be there day-to-day, who guests will see, whose hand the Mayor will shake, who Bruce Willis and Kevin Spacey will call when they need a table. That's you my boy, its' your turn now. Are you sincerely ready for all of this?" he said, still staring right at me. I could tell he had matured a lot over the last few years.

"I am. And I needn't say more." No more bullshit; let it begin.

"Then let's go. *The New York Times* has asked me for an exclusive. They want to know who it's gonna be. I'll call the editor and we'll set up an interview. Do you want to grab lunch first?" he asked, dialing his cell.

"Only if we need to; otherwise, I'd like to get on site and see the restaurant."

"It's still being built, but what is ready is beautiful. We'll spend the next month at Current, Maison and Trist working on recipes and you'll cook directly with me. We're going to be doing a ton of media profiling with you, getting your name out there. No one really knows who you are yet but you're so hot off your Boston stint that we think this will play well into our favor. We wanted an unknown, someone who could pump new life into this town just as Byzantine will do. That's why you're a perfect fit. You have more energy than anyone else in the game. You are going to be great Jack, I can feel it," Chef said, putting the phone up to his ear. He did reach the editor, and she was free to meet us for lunch right then and there. *The New York Times* editor was dropping what she was doing to come meet me. That's when I realized how big this was.

Her name was Diana—very cool, mid50s, silver hair, gray suit with a knee length skirt, extremely knowledgeable and to the point, but very easygoing. She spoke more to me then Chef Mike, and she wrote down everything: what I ordered, what I drank, I even think she wrote down when I went to the restroom. When lunch was over she paid the bill and we stood up to shake hands.

"It was very nice to meet you Chef; I know you will be a great success, especially working with Michael. I have known his work for many years. He is, in my opinion, the most talented Chef in the city. I look forward to watching your career grow as I watched his."

"Thank you, I look forward to seeing you again soon," I said making good eye contact.

"Oh don't worry Chef, you will, you will," she said as she left the table. Chef Mike turned to me.

"Good job Jack, very good job!" he said, sounding relieved.

"Really? Do you mean that? I've had a rough couple of days, and if you mean that it will go a very long way with me right now," I said, sort of wound up.

"Relax, my young prodigy, you did great," he said, patting my arm. "Maybe you were a little tight, is everything OK?"

I wanted to yell out *are you kidding me*? But instead, I just stated, "More than fine Chef. Can we go see the restaurant now?"

"With pleasure Chef, come on, I'll take you." I got chills down my spine because it was the first time I had heard *him* call me Chef, and mean it. I quickly followed like an excited puppy dog, though I would never show that. We had a car waiting for us outside the restaurant and we went directly to Byzantine.

The location could not have been better. We were on the border of the Financial District in a rare freestanding two-story building just a block away from Wall Street. It was like nothing I had ever seen before.

Everything was under construction but it must have been moving right along, because the whole block was full of contractors. Trucks were lined up on both sides of the street, to the point that police were directing traffic just to help the street flow. Our car was stuck in traffic so Mike and I just got out and walked. Everyone knew who he was; he stopped and said hello to a few of the guys and then there it was. It was enormous, as wide as the block was long. The face was glass—collapsible French doors with a large but understated sign that just said Byzantine in script letters. Brick surrounded the windows; it must have been a hundred-year-old building, but the finishes that were already in place were modern and world class, the only way Victor knew how to do things.

When we entered the space we put on hard hats. This was my first real "opening" from the very beginning, and if you have ever been part of a restaurant opening you know that it is brutal, and nothing ever goes according to plan. It opens much later than you thought, it's never on budget, staff is never trained for the initial sales you do, product sales are unpredictable, computers are programmed wrong, there are unexpectedly long waits, out of stock items, and it's a nightmare—that is, unless you're Victor Payne.

"No! Hell NO! You may think that's acceptable in your world, but your world is clearly a place ruled by weakness! In my world, we get our shit done on time, so if you can't get me my $120,000 hoods installed by Friday, then you're more replaceable than I thought! So what's it gonna be, guy? Can you do your job or what?" As we walked in we saw Victor on his phone; of course he wasn't wearing a hard hat, but rather a $6,000 Leonard Logsdail suit. He was screaming into his cell. He noticed me and said, "I've got more reliable people to talk to, call me in three minutes with a yes, or you're out." He hung up the phone and said, "Michael, Jack, I'm running out of heroes here, please tell me you got this." He hugged Mike.

"Victor, this is what we do, you are in good hands," Mike said, nonchalantly as ever.

Victor paused and licked his lips, "HA! Those are the best hands money can buy! I'm glad someone's got their head out of their ass, I'm not sure I can take any more of these imbeciles! Thank God I'm getting out of town tomorrow. I leave the rest to you Michael, I need a vacation!" he said, wiping the sweat off his brow.

"Where to this time, Victor?" Michael asked.

"Where else, Mikey? Vegas! I can't wait to take that town for all it's worth! I need some relaxation Mike, thank God the restaurants are doing the sales they're doing."

"You say it so modestly, Victor; we're New York's most profitable restaurant group," Michael said with confidence.

"Only because of you, my boy," he said, slapping Mike in the face. "And guys like this: So, Jack boy, how were the accommodations?" he said looking in my direction.

"Amazing Victor, I don't even know what to say."

"Say 'Hey Victor, great stuff, now let's make this property New York's best!'"

"That's why I'm here," I said folding my hands.

"You're damn right that's why you're here!" he said, looking at Mike. "Michael, get this boy to work. Let him know he's our number one draft pick, but draft day is over. No more smiling for the cameras, holding up your jersey and hugging Mommy and Daddy. It's time to see if you are worth all the money we spent on you. Time to see if you are who we think you are. Time to see if you can win us some games," he said, more seriously than I had ever heard him before.

Mike looked over at me, and before he could speak I said firmly, "Just show me to a kitchen, I'm ready to prove you right."

"You know, you never cease to amaze me! Look at this; do you know how much money is here? Do you know who's on the opening party guest list? Do you even understand the pressure?" He paused, gazing at me and coming closer. For a second I thought he was going to lose his cool, but not Victor, instead he said "HA! You're priceless! No pressure here, huh Mike! They're all just tickets to me! You got eight weeks kid. I'm off to the desert; good luck my boy, I couldn't put you in better hands. Make it work for

me baby, I've got something special for you when you do!"
he said as he left, then yelling something at a contractor as
his phone rang. He was tenacious as ever.

When Victor left, Michael took me on the whole tour
which left me in pure awe. We had four different dining
rooms, each unique: one was carpeted and decorated with
linen, chandeliers and art work, while the next was designed
with Edison light bulbs and an industrial feel. There was a
lounge, a whole room dedicated to greeting guests, and two
bars—one white marble seating about twenty and pouring
retro cocktails that were brought up to date, and the other
black granite and a full wine bar loaded with the best juice
from across the globe.

The main attraction was the two very large state-of-
the-art kitchens full of Sub-Zero and Wolf equipment;
three walk-in coolers per kitchen, all with clear glass doors;
blast chillers, sous vide machines and braising skillets; copper pans and molecular gastronomy tools. The shrink-wrap
was still on all the equipment, and the orange quarry tile
was still being laid piece by piece. The floor was loaded
with small wares and plate ware that were still in their boxes
so they didn't get dusty from the construction. Cooks who
were already working mostly spent their days scraping stick-
ers off of sauté pans and cleaning up when the contractors
quit for the day. It was like a chef's playground. Rumor had

it that the $20 million budget was an underestimate, and that even Victor was worried about the build-out cost.

The main dining room was a palace as well, with leather banquettes, top shelf liquor, silver, fine glassware, onyx tiles, expensive china, the world's best wines, thick copper menu bindings, lavish linens, and every luxury known to restaurants. It was something to be marveled at, like the Coliseum in Rome. It stood alone as one of a kind. It was near completion and I could already envision it full of New York's finest. The level of responsibility I faced was almost too much to grasp; I knew what I had to do. At the end of it all, the reclaimed cherry wood floors and the slowly distilled proprietor's reserve gin meant nothing if we failed to execute our food. It was all about the food, it always was, and that was why I was there. Success consumed me and this was the ultimate platform—and we were just getting started.

CHAPTER 23

WHEN NATURE CALLS

As the construction pressed forward and opening day drew closer, the media train didn't stop. We had interviews with every major publication in the city: the *Daily News*, *The New Yorker* and *The New York Times* were eating us up. We went national; *Bon Appetit* and *Food & Wine* did stories on us and what we were doing in New York. *New York Magazine* even put a picture of me, Mike and Victor on the cover of their March issue, which was amazing. We were just everywhere.

New York Times: "Wunderkind Set To Open Byzantine"

The Daily News: "The Next Harry Potter? No, It's Victor Payne's New Chef! 21-year-old set to open $40 million restaurant!"

USA Today: "Boston's Best Moves South! Jack Cahill to Open Byzantine."

It was crazy to read my name in the headlines like that, though I'd be lying if I said I didn't enjoy it. The weeks to come were like nothing I could have ever imagined; it was a media frenzy. I worked literally every day, up at 6am and asleep at 2am. I was burning hard. I had turned into a complete insomniac, but my life was moving so fast I did everything I could to keep up.

I worked at Maison a lot with Michael to perfect the dishes. Most days started in that kitchen around 7am. We were busy there, non-stop, but the kitchen was huge so it gave us a great place to work some research and development. We were playing with some of the world's best ingredients: Hudson Valley foie gras, Kobe beef from Japan, sea urchin, bone marrow, oysters, caviar, we had it all. We tested recipes all day, working on presentations and garnishes, making sure they were appropriate and priced right. Money was never the top concern for Victor; he wanted quality regardless but we always had to pay attention to costs and profits.

We always focused on how a dish worked, and the mechanics of a line. Our main goal was execution; could we make each dish to the necessary quality and put out more than 1,000 dishes a day? Mike knew how big the machine of a kitchen was—it was a lot of very fragile moving parts. If he and I were making every dish it would be easy, but we weren't. We had a huge crew at Byzantine, almost 200 total, one of the biggest crews in New York. When you have a crew that big, you have to put systems in place to make sure you are consistent. Mike always said the highest compliment a chef could be paid in a single word is consistent. He knew his shit and he was right: it has to be great and it has to be the same every time. Each meal, whether you're there weekly or yearly, it always needs to be the same. The guests remember great food, but they remember it even clearer when they return and it's different. Better or worse, it's still different. Mike always said he'd rather be a "B" all of the time than an "A" sometimes and a "C" other times. He was extremely wise and sure of himself.

Usually the development portion of our day ended around 6 or 7. We worked at it hard for about 12 hours, non-stop, barely taking time to eat. We documented everything; Mike had a kitchen scribe there writing down his recipes and tweaking them as he went. When they were complete they were typed, photographed, filed and printed for use. When we wrapped that part of the day, there was always an interview. The media was really turning me on; I was getting addicted to the spotlight. We were doing an interview with the *Daily News* once and Michael, who liked the press but didn't love it, said fewer than ten words. I did all the talking about the restaurant. When the interview concluded, the reporter asked playfully, "So Chef, what's for dinner tonight?"

"Why don't you meet me at my place around midnight and I'll show you," I said boldly.

"Sounds great — see you then," she said seductively as she stood up and left. Mike gave me a look of disapproval.

"What? Does it always have to be all work no play?" I said gruffly.

"When there's this much on the line, yes, I think it does," he said, standing up as well. "See you tomorrow at 6:30am. Let's meet at Byzantine, our kitchens are ready." He looked very tired. I couldn't blame him; we were working our asses off and getting no sleep, and it wasn't getting any better.

That reporter did end up meeting me at my place. I made a quick and easy dinner, roast game hen, soft polenta and porcini mushrooms, and an amazing cabernet. She must have taken two bites before climbing across the table at me. We had a wild night. I was having many wild nights behind the scenes, trying to keep Mike out of it, but this one became blatant the next day when the headlines came out: "Byzantine Chef is Real Deal"

That may not sound like a big deal, but the article was very flattering to me and there was a lot of inside scoop that no one else knew. What made matters worse was that there was no mention of Mike or Victor in the whole column, only me. That was sort of a slap in the face to the guys who got me there, and Mike knew she'd come on to me. This had potential to be bad.

"Hey Jack," he said as I got to Byzantine the next morning, right on time. He was writing menus with all the day's papers next to him. He was in his checkered chef pants and a t-shirt, drinking coffee.

"Chef," I said evenly as I sat down across from him. "What's the game plan today?"

"We need to develop our timeline. We're now just two weeks from opening. I know we're ready, and it's time to get the crew in here full-time, stock this place with food, and get ready for premier night. Victor's back next week and I want this place running like a well-oiled machine by then, with room to spare. We need to focus harder than ever. Let's try to keep the late nights to a minimum and buckle down. This is what you have been trained for; this is why you're here." He pulled out the *Daily News* and placed it down in front of me. "Not for this," he said calmly.

"Yes Chef," I said, but reluctantly. It was my first real piece of solo success since I got to New York. I liked it, and I actually thought he was resentful.

"Jack, are we clear on this? Your objective is the restaurant's success, nothing more," he said, taking away the paper.

"Of course Chef, I don't care about any of this. I care about Byzantine. Now say no more and let's get to work," I said. I brushed it off, but I did care; I liked it a lot and wanted more. I wanted my name in the paper every day; I wanted to be on TV, to be known throughout the world. I was loving the attention, and was beginning to crave it more and more.

Mike and I worked all day developing station maps, working on the flow of food, where we would put what ingredient, what station would prepare what dish, behind the scenes stuff that no one ever sees. So many people fail in this business because they lack the forethought and preparation; they just open the doors one day and hope it all goes well but it rarely ever does. That's why there are so many mediocre restaurants out there. I wasn't going to let that happen here.

At the end of another long day Mike and I were leaving Byzantine and we ran into a familiar face.

"Hey Michael, how's it going in there?" It was movie star Jim Carrey.

"Hey Jim, oh you know, it's a lot of work right now but it's all worth it in the end," Mike said smoothly. He was always a cool operator. "Jim, this is Jack Cahill, he's my new chef here." I extended my hand.

"Pleased to meet you," he said, shaking my hand. "I read about you guys all the time. I can't wait for you to open, you know I live just a few blocks from here," he said, pointing over his shoulder.

"Yeah that's right, you live in Victor's building," Mike said.

"YES! Victor, oh he's a character. Nicest guy though, he lives just a few floors up from me in the penthouse. Little bastard just beat me to it! I'm going to grab a drink, you guys want to come?"

"No, I don't think so Jim but thanks, we have another long day tomorrow," Mike said, shaking it off and putting his hands in his coat pockets. In the old days, Mike would never pass up an opportunity for a night like that. He was different these days, not as much fun as he once was— all business, all the time.

"Oh come on, I'm dying to hear about the menu, my treat?" he said, insisting on it. "Come on, we'll swap Victor stories. You think I was in *When Nature Calls*, woooo you got to hear some of the sounds that come out of his place!" he said, laughing it up.

"OK, one drink and then we have to get going," Mike said, looking in my direction.

"Great! Come on, let's have some fun!" Jim said. We followed him to a busy bar around the corner. I couldn't believe I was going out for drinks with Jim Carrey. When we walked in no one really noticed us at first, but the longer we sat, the more people were looking in our direction, pointing and whispering.

"So boys, I had a scotch with Victor last week and he was telling me about the place, sounds unbelievable! We need something new in this town; it's all the same shit everywhere you go. He says you're a breath of fresh air Jack." Chef's head was all over the place; he looked uncomfortable.

"Yeah, well, I mean thank you, but I don't know about that. I'm just trying to keep up with this guy," I said, grabbing Mike's arm.

"Oh he's good. I remember meeting him back at Duet before he was the king of New York, back when he was just a little unknown chef. Then he did the Big Raw Bar. He was talented even before his Dexter House days," Jim said, sipping his martini. "Ah! That's good! So tell me, what's the food all about?"

"We're doing food from all around the world Jim, a lot of classics brought back to life, modernized food made with high end ingredients," Mike said, sort of sounding bored when he described it. No wonder I took control of that interview. I could see he was tired though; I guess I couldn't blame him.

"Huh, well with you on top of things Mike, I'm sure it's going to be great!" Jim said, looking past Mike at a couple of girls at the bar. Mike looked over his shoulder to see what he was looking at.

"Well Jim, thanks for the drink but we need to get going," he said, standing up and putting his coat on. I didn't move.

"Oh come on Mike, you just got here! OK, fine, what about you Jack? You're not making me fly solo here are you?" he said, spreading his arms out. Mike looked at me like it was my choice.

"No, of course not Jim, let's get another round!" I said, finishing my cocktail. Mike nodded at me and turned to Jim, "Thanks Jim, always a pleasure," he said, shaking his hand and giving him a half hug.

"Good to see you Mike, hey I'll see you in couple of weeks, right?"

"Yeah of course, it's going to be great you'll see. Good night guys." He put his hands back in his pocket and left.

"Geez, that guy's uptight huh?" Jim said, rolling his eyes. He was only half kidding of course.

"He can be, but he's a great guy and a very talented chef," I said in his defense.

"Ummmm," Jim was sipping his martini, "no doubt, I mean no doubt, he's the best. Just never loosens up anymore, guess its hard to in that line of work, although you seem pretty relaxed. Why are you so cool about everything?" he asked, eating an olive and still half looking at the girls at the bar, who were clearly looking back.

I looked over my shoulder. "Do you want me to go get them?" I asked smoothly.

"Haha, please, don't get up." He stuck his hand in the air and they came running.

The night just kept going from there. We drank all night and sang songs with the piano player. Twenty people were around us by night's end and each of us left with one of the girls. Jim and I exchanged phone numbers when we went our separate ways outside. I walked home with a girl on my arm, down the streets of New York City, feeling on top of the world again. I didn't even know her name but she was completely into me. It was insane, but I was just enjoying it. I took her back to my place around 3am and didn't sleep a wink. We left together around 6am because I had to meet Mike for work.

"You look like hammered shit," he said to me as I walked in, on time but barely.

"Chef, how could you not have stayed last night, it was a blast! I mean, Ace Ventura kind of a blast!" I said, still very excited and still buzzed.

Mike shook his head at me, "This is what I'm talking about Jack. You're a mess, you need to get your shit together and fast," he said very seriously.

"I got this Chef, let's get to work. Don't worry about me, I can handle all this and then some," I said firmly in return.

"You're starting to believe what they're writing about you out there. Get your head out of the clouds and keep it out of your ass. There's too much on the line here Jack." He was getting upset; I'd never seen him upset.

I snapped out of it, "OK Chef, you're right, I'm sorry." I shook my head to wake up. "I'm ready, let's get to work."

He dropped it and we got back to work. I must have drunk ten cups of coffee that day. I don't know how I did it but I got through the day, and was actually quite productive. Mike called it quits around 7pm and I went straight home because I was exhausted. I laid down on the couch and turned on the Yankees game when I noticed the light blinking on my answering machine.

"Hey Jackie, it's Mom, just calling to check in. Haven't heard from you in a while but wanted to let you know we love you very much. Give us a call sometime, OK? Love you Jack!"

"Hi Jack, it's Miranda! I had a great time with you last night, was hoping you were free later, give me a call, I left you a present under your pillow! Later!"

"Jack, it's Travis. Just checking in, making sure you're OK! We miss you up here, give us a call and let us know how life's treating ya!"

"Um . . . hi Jack, it's Karen." I stopped pacing and looked right at the machine; I almost got whiplash, I turned around so fast. "Look, I feel awful about the way we left things. I didn't want it to be like this. You don't have to call me back but I wanted to wish you well and tell you I was thinking about you. Best of luck super chef, I miss you very much." Beep.

My mouth curled up and my muscles got tense. What the hell was she doing to me? Or was it me—was I to blame? She showed up thinking we could get a drink and talk and I expected her to drop everything, move to New York and just be with me? I picked up the phone and then put it down. I picked it up again then put it down again. I walked over to the mirror and stared, then I threw the phone at it, shattering it to pieces!

I screamed and clenched my fists before I realized I was bleeding. I was so tired, so burnt out, and now this. I couldn't deal. I went to bed and fell right in. Under my pillow was Miranda's thong; I looked at for a second and just broke down. *Who am I? What am I doing?* I felt like I was falling completely apart. I was so wiped out I just fell asleep for the next 10 hours. It was the most sleep I had gotten in months.

CHAPTER 24

THE BLUE ROOM

Paparazzi had taken photos of Jim and me that night and they were published in *Inside*, the *Enquirer*, the *Times*, and we even made a few TV shows—no big story or anything, but my phone never stopped ringing as a result. I had become very popular but I'd told Mike I would calm down so I had, at least for the two weeks leading up to opening night.

We had a stellar VIP guest list: the governor, the mayor, celebrities, athletes, it was going to be the social event of the year. I was back on top of my game. Mike never said a word; I think he was just happy to see me without bags under my eyes for a change. We had been working so hard and suddenly opening night was upon us. Victor wanted to do something special, so he had the team from Current come to the restaurant and make dinner for us. The irony of Billy now in the kitchen cooking for me, it felt great. All the top people from Byzantine—Michael, Victor, the sous chefs, floor managers, and the general manager Aaron—were at the dinner. Everyone brought spouses or partners but me; I was the lone wolf as always.

Dinner was served in the Blue Room, which was decorated in cobalt blue glass with slick metallic gray accents. White chairs and stainless steel trimmings made it very modern, and long window treatments helped maintain the classic feel. All the dining rooms were amazing, but I knew Victor favored this one, maybe because it had the scotch cupboard which held about $250,000 in rare scotch. The vibe was great; loud modern era music was cranking and mirrors and sensual artwork decorated the walls. It was very cutting-edge. Everyone was well-dressed. It was quite a treat to be there that night. It had been a long journey and a lot of work, so it was nice to relax and be on the other side of the table for a change.

For a few minutes, as everyone gathered around the table dressed in their best, I couldn't help but stop and look around for a minute to take it all in. How far I had come. My peers were the top names in my field, and I was now here comfortably among them. Our general manager Aaron had worked all over Europe and had once been the Maître D at Bocuse in France. In the States he'd opened and developed James Beard Award-winning restaurants in San Francisco and Chicago. He was always well-dressed and was vastly knowledgeable. He was also a total pompous asshole, but debonair no doubt. Victor had assembled one hell of a team.

"A toast!" Victor said, standing up and holding up his glass. "To all of you, you are the reason I am here, you are the reason for all of this. I owe you thanks and give you your due praise," he said, bowing dramatically.

"Hear, hear!" Aaron said, raising his glass. We had been in many meetings together as of late and the more I got to know him, the less I liked him. He took a sip of champagne and wiped his mouth with his napkin. "Excuse me dear, I'll be right back," he said, looking at his cell phone as it rang. He quickly left the table.

"I swear he'd fuck that thing if he could," Aaron's wife said. Although we were sitting next to each other, I'd been eating and not looking in her direction. At first I didn't even realize she was talking to me.

"I'm sorry, were you talking to me?" I said, finishing my bite.

"Yes, I'm sorry," she said, laughing slightly. "I said I swear he spends more time on that phone than he does with me," she said, rubbing her neck. She was a very striking woman, tall and thin, with long flowing blonde hair, blue eyes, and great skin. She was wearing a very flattering low cut black dress and sexy pair of white stilettos. I hadn't met her until now.

I was mildly confused, and it took me a second to answer. "Now that you mention it, he is on it quite often," I said, reaching for my champagne.

"I'm Ava, you must be the guy everyone's talking about," she said, looking interested in my response.

"I'm Jack, I'm not sure what they're saying but I'm sure only half of it's true," I said, looking at my food and not her.

She burst out laughing. "Ah, you are charming!" she said flirtatiously.

"Goddamn people can never get it right!" Aaron said furiously as he returned to the table. "I've got to go sweetheart, the guys at Maison have issues. Why do I even try to relax!" he said, slugging back his champagne. Aaron was still in charge of Maison until we were opened, and his passing of the baton to the new general manager was not going as smoothly as he had hoped. "Victor, duty calls," he said, shaking his hand.

"Oh yes Aaron, see you tomorrow," Victor said, barely acknowledging him. Aaron was always trying to kiss Victor's ass but Victor never gave him the time of day, despite his credentials.

"Honey," he came over to Ava and gave her a kiss on the lips, "Chef, everyone, good night and I will see you all tomorrow." He waved and flew out of there as quickly as he'd come. I wasn't a huge fan of his.

"Guess I'll just stay here, darling," she said to herself as she finished her champagne. She looked lonely and sad, so I had to say something.

"Being stag has its advantages; at least we don't have to listen to his God awful jokes for the rest of the night." Aaron told the worst jokes, and lots of them.

She slowly turned her head in my direction and smiled, "Yes, he does tell terrible jokes now, doesn't he." She stuck out her glass and the waiter refilled it. She was smiling at me.

"Some of the worst ever," I said sitting back, still only making partial eye contact. "How long have you been married?" I asked as I took another bite.

"Two years," she said, sipping her champagne. She was drinking awfully fast. "And you? Where's your special someone?"

"Right there," I said, pointing at Victor. He noticed, tipped his glass, smiled, and raised his eyebrows.

She smiled, "You are funny. So, I read about you all the time, must be hard being a celebrity chef," she said, turning toward me.

"I wouldn't know; I'm just trying to do the best I can for the team."

"Oh please, I see you on TV, in the magazines, you're a very, how should I say, hot item right now." She slipped her hand down onto my leg and I froze mid-bite. I slowly put my fork down and leaned back. "More champagne?" she said as I looked in her direction.

I swallowed so hard it made a sound. "Sure, bring it on," I said calmly. The waiter brought it over to us.

"Leave the bottle please," she said to him. "This night just got much better," she said flirtatiously.

"Guess we'll see," I responded coolly.

The night was a hit. Around midnight it was breaking up and people were heading to the doors. I had spoken with Ava for most of the night. She talked about what a mistake she'd made marrying Aaron, saying that she'd never loved him. She asked me repeatedly about a lady in my life and I kept dodging the subject. She was very cool and wildly sexy. A little too wild, in fact.

Victor was at the door saying goodbye to everyone as they were leaving, Ava and I got to the door at the same time.

"Goodnight gorgeous," he said, giving Ava a kiss on the cheek. "That Aaron is a lucky son of a bitch!" he said, waving goodbye.

He pulled me in as we shook hands. "So are you," he whispered. "Do us both a favor, be careful with this one, OK kid?" he said with a serious face. He had both hands on my face. I knew he had noticed Ava and me aggressively flirting, and I could tell he was looking out for me. I felt like he had my back. He was beyond my mentor now; I emulated him and he knew it. He never directly gave an order—he was 100% free will, just don't make the wrong choice. I heeded his warning with my ears and eyes wide open.

"Nothing to worry about there, game day tomorrow. I'm off to rest up," I said as I buttoned my coat. "Good night Victor, and thanks again for a great night." I smiled at him endearingly and headed out.

"Good night kiddo," he said with fatigue in his voice. He paused and then turned to his date – always a different one – "Come on baby, I need a steam and a night cap." I saw him give one last look in my direction as he turned away.

Ava was on the corner hailing a cab, as were a few other guests. I was walking in her direction. "Which way you headed?" she asked me.

"I'm just a few blocks away by the park, right on the corner of Albany and South End," I said, popping my collar up. It was a little chilly that evening.

"Wanna share a cab with me? I mean, I'm heading that way anyway," she said, tilting her head. She looked awfully good in the moon light.

As tempted as I was, I was dedicated to tomorrow. "No thank you Ava. This was a great night, thanks for the company," I said. "I think I'm gonna walk tonight."

"Too bad, I thought this was gonna be a fun night," she said unbuttoning her top button and licking her lips. Everyone else had already gotten taxis and we were the only two left. Looking around, we were the only people as far as the eye could see.

I hesitated because she looked so sexy but I said, "It was, thanks for the conversation." Ava was ridiculously hot, super model hot. My heart was pounding and I wasn't thinking with my head. I had to get out of there so I gave her a wave, "Good night Ava." I turned and walked into the night.

I lived just four blocks from the restaurant, so it probably took me 10 minutes to get home. It was late, and I was tired but excited for the next day so I had to pass that up. Besides, it was Aaron's wife and as much as I disliked him, I didn't want to put myself in that position . . . though I'd be lying if I said I didn't regret it the whole walk home. As I approached my building a cab pulled up. It stopped just as I arrived, and sure enough, there was Ava. She had rebuttoned her coat all the way to the top.

"I forgot to give you something," she said as she got out of the cab. She took three very slow steps toward me, holding her arms behind her back. "Put out your hand," she said seductively.

She pulled her dress out from behind her and placed in my outstretched hand. She must have taken it off in the cab. I was instantly and ferociously turned on.

"That's a very nice gift," I said, swallowing again. She was an incredibly sexy woman. "I would like to give you something in return," I said, looking into her deep blue eyes. I caved, now I wanted her so badly.

"So come give it to me," she said, walking up my stairs. I was done for. We went up to my place and as soon as we walked in the door she slid off her coat. She was completely naked, wearing only those white stilettoes and necklace. "Where's your bedroom, Chef?" she said, biting her thumbnail and smiling at me. Her body was gorgeous and I was so turned on every muscle in my body was tingling. I didn't say anything, I just pointed, swallowed and followed her there. Watching her walk one foot in front of the other, naked in those heels, was just explosive. It was an extremely erotic night and it lasted for hours. Even after it calmed down, she stayed for a little while and we just had a few laughs. Around 5am she said she needed to get going. She was very cool the whole time, funny and charming. I sincerely liked her, but this couldn't continue. She kissed me and said, "You were great, I'd love to do this again very soon." She slid down the bed, now fully dressed, and waved goodbye. "Call me," she said as the door closed behind her. The sound of that door closing was her leaving and all sorts of problems walking in.

I sat there in my bed with nothing but the sounds of New York in my ears. I looked around the room and thought about what had just happened. Now that she was gone and the champagne was wearing off, it was starting to sink in. "Fuck me," I said. I put a pillow over my head, closed my tired eyes, and went to sleep.

CHAPTER 25

GAME DAY

When I woke up the next morning I had a feeling of great concern. I showered it away, grabbed a coffee at Dean and Deluca, and headed to the restaurant. On the rack I saw the day's paper: "Byzantine Green Lit to Open. Owner Victor Payne assures us the opening night gala will be one for the history books. He and his young superstar chef are poised to make history!" Nothing like a little pressure to start my day! I walked into work in my usual fashion—jeans, flannel shirt, coat, my shoulder bag, and my clogs. My uniform was pressed and hanging in my office. I thought I was first in but Victor had beaten me to it.

"Game day my boy!" he said, giving me a hug. "You ready to make history?" He put one arm around me.

"Beyond ready," I said with confidence, but I was looking around to see if Aaron had arrived. That was the last thing I needed on my mind.

"HA! Don't I know it! You have been doing amazing work. Your food is so refined and your leadership is at its peak. You are ready my boy, this I know!" he said confidently. "OK, I'm going about my way, have Mike call me when he gets in. Good luck, see you at party time!" he said, patting me on the back as he left. He looked around at his baby as he sauntered out. You could see he was slightly nervous but full of pride. He had all the faith in the world in me, and suddenly I had this whole other distraction to deal with. Looking over my shoulder, I headed to the office and got changed.

As I slipped into my coat I was overwhelmed with its inscription: Byzantine, Jack Cahill, Executive Chef. It was my first executive chef coat. Coats are a big deal to chefs, like medals to soldiers; it means something if you don the title on your chest. It filled me with pride that I was there, that we made it, that Byzantine was alive.

I entered the dark kitchen and turned on the lights, flipping the switches one at a time. As section by section illuminated, I took just a second to look at each one with admiration. Our kitchen was amazing. Our equipment was polished, our herb bins were alive and growing, our uniforms were pressed, and our china was new and sparkling. It was something special to be the first one in that day, though my crew was minutes behind me so I started getting us hot. Unit by unit I turned everything on, one oven after another, one fryer after another, just making sure everything was up and running. I headed to my station, center middle—the middle of two middles, everything converged there. I made my commands through a microphone but each station had a computer that automatically told them what to do, so it was much less verbal. I only needed to speak when something wasn't happening the way it was supposed to. My set-up was also much less involved, all plates left their stations complete; this was a much bigger operation and it was all about overseeing, not as much doing. As chef, my job was done in the research and training phase. It was my job to make sure the crew knew what they were doing and I felt like they did. I was truly prepared and very organized.

My mind, however, was a different story. I was constantly looking over my shoulder for Aaron, though you wouldn't know it. I looked focused on what I was doing. I'd fucked up, but was hopeful that Ava wouldn't say anything to him. I just kept my head down and concentrated, but it was much harder to do that than it used to be. I heard voices coming from around the corner.

"So we'll put Derek Jeter at table 25 and switch it for Johnny Depp's table, I know Derek will appreciate the view." It was Aaron, looking all business. "Chef, how are we feeling?" he asked me.

"Feeling well Aaron and you?" I said, organizing some pans. Cooks were slowly trickling in around me to get their day started.

"You're not gonna believe what my wife said to me," he said, leaning in. I completely froze dead in my tracks. "She comes home and says, 'hey honey, when you first saw me naked, what went through your mind?' I said I wanted to fuck your brains out and suck your tits dry. She takes off her clothes last night and says, 'what's going through your mind now?' I said, looks like I did a pretty good job!" he said, laughing. Son of a bitch was just making one of his lame jokes. He left as soon as he finished, screaming at the other manager to wait up for him. He didn't know. I let out the deepest breath of my life. I was in the clear. I clapped my hands with pride, "All right boys, let's get this place set up double time, huge night, and I want time to spare for pre-meal. All stations use your prep lists and submit them to me by 2:30pm. If you are not finished, we'll get you finished. Now HUSTLE!" I was fired up.

We banged out prep like lightning; $20,000 in product came in that day alone and we shredded it like it was nothing. Mike was on scene keeping an eye on things, and he seemed very pleased with my progress. I was in full command and he knew it. Aaron went to Maison to tie up some loose ends, and Victor had come back early. The team was in full force, the building was surrounded by customers waiting to come in, and the media were waiting to see celebrities as they arrived. Our guest list was packed. We were going to do record-breaking sales for the industry; we had the potential to do $150,000 a day, huge numbers, and I had it fully under control.

My staff submitted their lists, I did my line checks, and so did Mike. My sous chefs were in position on time. We gathered the huge 200-person staff together for our first pre-meal. There were so many people that we needed to use the microphone. Michael began.

"Well, I don't want to take up a lot of your time, Aaron and Jack will do most of the talking, but I wanted to wish everyone well. This restaurant is groundbreaking. This night is historic for our industry. I will be here to help every step of the way. We don't expect it to be perfect but we do expect you to do what you've trained to do. I am proud to be here with all of you tonight, I am proud to be your Chef, and I am looking forward to this and many more great nights to come. Byzantine means complex, but let's make this easy tonight, OK people? Best of luck, and let's stay focused," he said, passing me the microphone. He was a man of few words but people liked to hear him talk.

"Thank you Chef. It's we who are proud to be here with you tonight. We are all thankful for what you have done for us. You're a great mentor and a true friend." I looked at him with the utmost pride. I couldn't believe how far we had come together. "OK, so I want to talk a little about tonight's flow. Ideally, what I would like is—"

"You son of a bitch!" I heard someone scream furiously. It was Aaron, pushing through the crowd. He was totally red in the face, literally pushing servers aside to get to me. "*You mother **fucker!***" Boom! He hit me right in the face, knocking me off my step stool and onto the ground. "Who the fuck do you think you are!" he said, choking me. It was so unexpected that I didn't even have time to fight back. Mike and a couple of servers ripped him off of me.

"What are you, fucking *crazy*?" Mike said to him. "Get the fuck out of here, you're fired!" he said to Aaron, who was breathing so heavily you could see his body moving.

"Mike, that little shit fucked Ava!" he said, wiping his mouth with his sleeve. He had cut his lip when he fell and blood was running down his chin.

Mike looked over at me, "Tell me that's not true?" But he knew it was, I could see it in his eyes.

I cracked my neck and touched my eye, which I could already feel was swelling. I nodded shamefully, unable to look him in the eye. I saw Victor calmly walk into the kitchen, staying out of it. He watched this unfold with his hands in his pockets. The place was dead silent to the point of eeriness.

Mike was looking back and forth at Aaron and me. We were both waiting for him to say something. Finally, he looked at me and said, "Get out of here." I looked up slowly at him. "You heard me *get the hell out of here*! You're fired!" It was the first and only time I ever heard him yell. The staff was stunned. I looked at Victor in hopes of getting some support but said nothing and made no expression. I looked around the room at the hundreds of faces, the faces of the people who worked for me; sadly, I hadn't even taken the time to learn half their names. I saw Aaron still breathing heavily and shaking. My cooks looked away from me. I had no choice but to leave. I did it very slowly, hoping Mike or Victor would say something to me, but they didn't. They just let me walk out in silence. I went to the office and took off my coat that I had just put on for the first time. I hung it up just as I'd found it, touched the logo, took one last look at it, and left. As I did, I heard Victor call my name.

"Ain't easy being on top sometimes," he said as he approached me. He was walking as calmly as ever.

"Victor, I am so sorry," I said with total shame on my face.

"Let me tell you something kiddo, if every angry husband whose wife I was with came after me, let's just say I might not be here to tell about it," he said, putting his hand on my shoulder. "But Mike's not gonna be able to stand for this, so I have to support him. Besides, when this hits the papers I'm gonna have to say I did the right thing." He was unusually supportive.

"Victor, I—

"Let's leave it at this kid. You weren't ready, you have what it takes but you weren't ready to handle what comes along with it. It's OK, I wasn't either when I was your age. Go back out into the world and get your shit together. I tried to force this and I'm sorry." He was rubbing my shoulder. "This doesn't have to be goodbye; it just needs to be I'll see you later." He smiled at me as I looked up. He was right. I guess wasn't ready. Billy was right, Mike was right. It all came so fast and I think a piece of me was left behind that night in Boston. "Use the apartment for a week or two, get some yourself together, but then I gotta ask you to give it up," he said, putting his hands back into his pockets. "I got to go kiddo. I've got my opportunities and they lie behind that door. Yours lie out here, somewhere in this world. Ask yourself this question: which ones do I want to pursue . . . and go do it." He turned and headed back. I watched him, still shaken up as he headed back in the back door. He never turned around again, but as he entered I heard him shout, one last time to me, "Opportunities my boy! Opportunities."

CHAPTER 26

NOT THIS TIME

The days that followed were the most difficult of my life, dark in most ways but enlightening in others. I was so used to my pace that I didn't know how to occupy my time. My pace — I say that as if it were ever truly mine; it was Victor's pace, it wasn't my own. After nights of drinking away the shock that was my new reality, I knew I needed to create a pace of my own, but what was that? Who was I? Victor's words haunted me, missed opportunities and I just missed a huge one, in fact I had missed quite a few. I tried to wash away those words, as well as my pain, with anything I could get my hands on, wine, tequila, scotch, whiskey, anything to make the echo's in my head stop, but they didn't, if anything they got louder. I wondered if my real missed opportunity was not saying something to Mike. Had I grimaced and fled prematurely, or was that what was supposed to happen to my life? I was scared. I'd never felt scared in my entire life. Fear was unfamiliar, but it was now everywhere in my world. Paranoia and depression haunted me as well. I was at the bottom, somewhere I was sure I would never be.

Days went by slowly, but they still went by. As they passed, the harsh reality of my life started settling in. I hadn't saved a penny, I didn't have a job, and I didn't have anywhere to live. The only thing I had was my reputation, and I only had that because what had happened never went public. I looked every day, but it wasn't in the papers, magazines or the internet; it was nowhere. Byzantine was though, just as hot as they knew it would be. Mike's name was back in the headlines and mine just seem to disappear. Victor once told me he thought of Mike like fire insurance: not something you need every day, but when the flames are on you he's right. Mike was reliable and strong. He'd grown over the years and he tried to warn me of my ways. He tried to share his experience with me, to pass on his knowledge so I could learn from his mistakes in order to keep me out of trouble. He was right, I wasn't ready, and he'd known it. Maybe they were all right. Maybe Karen was right too; maybe we weren't ready to be together. Maybe we never would be. It became clear that she'd been right about that. *You were right Karen, I was wrong, we weren't ready.* I'd treated her like shit about that cold hard fact. I know she felt horrible about everything, and I hadn't had the courtesy to return her call. Even when I turned my back on her, she was still there for me. A wrong I might never be able to right.

Victor was there for me too, even in the aftermath of Byzantine. We never spoke, but I knew he was the one who kept me from public humiliation, he kept the whole mess out of the media's eye. He was that powerful and calculating.

Lamenting and worrying day in and day out was doing me absolutely no good. I couldn't keep feeling sorry for myself; these days opened my eyes to so many aspects of my life. Stepping back gave me true perspective about what was important, where I was, what I was doing, and where I needed to go. With my days numbered in New York and no time to pull something together I had no choice but to pack up and head back home. As much as I didn't want to leave the city, I was broke and the only option I had was to go to my parents, at least briefly to buy me some time.

My parent's house looked exactly the same as it did when I was last there years ago. They were both home when I arrived, I knocked on the front door and my Mother opened it.

"Oh my gosh!" my mother screamed. "My baby's home! Silvio, Jackie's here!" she screamed in complete jubilation "What are you doing here baby?"

"I'm back Ma, and I missed you guys!" I said with a smile on my face. I hadn't seen them in so long.

My dad came walking down the stairs. "Wait, when you say you're back, you mean like to live here with us?" he said, kidding around . . .but he so wasn't.

"Maybe for a couple of days but I'll find somewhere fast, don't worry about that. If that's OK, of course," I said happily.

"Of course that's ok, whatever you need! Come in baby, are you hungry, thirsty, you need to tell us what's been going on, why are you here?" she asked in her nurturing way.

"It's a long story guys, I don't even know where to begin."

I sat down and ate lunch with my parents. I told them about the rise and fall of their son the chef. I told them about Boston and New York, I showed them my awards, the newspapers and magazines. I told them that it was time to right my wrongs and to undo the mess I had made. I knew what I needed to do to start over, it wouldn't happen overnight but I knew what I needed to do.

Slowly but surely over the next few weeks I started to put it back together. I found a small apartment, not much but it was mine. There I drew my line in the sand and said from that moment on I was moving forward and never going back. When you reach the bottom the whole world looks different. You see everything so much more clearly; you realize what you need in life and what you don't; and you realize who is there for you and who is not. I was determined to reach the top again but this time I would do it all right. I'd gotten so caught up in the glamour and glitz of Victor, New York, Boston, and the media, that I had forgotten what was important to me, what was important to my life. I did love all of those things, and perhaps one day I would have them again, but I realized that life requires more balance. I didn't need to alienate everything else exclusively for them. I was starting to get that feeling again, the feeling of autonomy, and the feeling that with hard work and uncompromised dedication, I could accomplish anything. I'd proved it once, and it was now time to prove it again.

The first job I took cooking again was at a little 40-seat restaurant called The Creek Side Bistro on Wappinger's Creek just outside of Pleasant Valley. It had a tiny balcony overlooking the creek that sat about 20 more people. It was a cute and charming place, but basic: wooden chairs, white tablecloths, old school fireplace, and pictures of flowers and wine bottles on the wall. It was just outside town, and was a popular local place. Our kitchen was open to the dinning room and there was a bell on the door that rang every time it opened. I always looked up to see who walked in the door—maybe it would be an old friend or classmate I hadn't seen in some time, I was always curious to see who it was.

After a few months of working there, the local paper *The Pleasant Valley Journal* wrote an article about me that read, "Star Chef Returns Home." It included my picture; it was on page seven but still a nice mention. It was far from the cover of the *New York Times* but it was something, my rise had begun again, I was back on my path and this time I would stay on it. I would be focused and I would be patient. This time, there would be no missed opportunities. Victor would be proud, I know he would; I knew Victor, and I was proud to say I knew him.

Great people worked at the Creek Side, salt of the earth, small town folk with small town ambitions. I stayed humble and did my job. They liked me. I worked hard and helped everyone around me. I was a mentor, but in the Mike Roderick style of leading by example. The food was so basic but I loved being there, and I always made sure to show my gratitude. They gave me a job when I needed it most and I was truly appreciative to have it.

Though the Creek Side wasn't exactly where I wanted to be it was helping me get my feet back under me. I couldn't afford New York, so as usual I worked hard day in and day out to save money wherever I could. I stopped drinking and stayed focused on my new climb, I would reach the top again, that much I promised myself, but for now at 22 years old, I was where I was, and I was more then content with that.

One day, after a busy lunch I was wiping down my cutting board, enjoying the feeling of being able to concentrate again, to find the joy in a good service the way I once had relishing in the simplicity of it all. It was a gorgeous spring day and the restaurant was just clearing out, only a few couples remained. I leaned down to wipe the front of my station when I heard the bell on the front door ring. I picked up my head to look as I always did, only to see the most beautiful woman walk through the door. It was Karen, looking as amazing as ever, wearing a light green sundress, flip-flops, and a yellow wrap around her shoulders holding an issue of *The Pleasant Valley Journal* in her hand. She looked around smiling for a moment before our eyes met. When they did, we both froze to look at each other, and it was undoubtedly the most powerful moment of my life. I stood upright straightening my apron, my heart pounding out of my chest. I couldn't believe she was there, right there, standing in front of me. As she raced towards me, I reached out to grab her wrapping my arms as tightly around her as I could. We held each other close pausing only to take a breath and let it all sink in. She had come back just as she said she would. She was right all along, she was right about everything. Timing was never our thing but seeing her there made me feel that maybe, just maybe, this was *finally* our time. I had never been more certain of anything in my life. With her in my arms I instantly felt whole, Karen was the most important thing to me, she always had been and I somehow lost sight of that along the way. Victor always said that life was defined by missed opportunities. Missed opportunities. . . not this time.

"Even when they get cut down, the tough ones grow back stronger than ever."
Michael Roderick

ABOUT THE AUTHOR

Nick Rabar is a career Chef with 20 years of industry experience. He is the Chef / Owner of Avenue N American Kitchen and The Pantry both located in his home town of Rumford Rhode Island. He is married to wife Tracy and is the proud father of three sons, Jackson, Parker and Wynn. When he's not in the kitchen, Nick is the infallible host of the Emmy Nominated lifestyle and cooking show, Nick Rabar: Chef 2 Go. Before deciding to pen The Cold Side of the Grill, his work was featured in multiple local and national publications. His career has been decorated with numerous awards including being named "Best and Brightest Young American Chefs" by Spirit Magazine and "Chef of the Year" by the Rhode Island Hospitality Association. His flagship restaurant Avenue N was named "Best Neighborhood Restaurant in New England" by Yankee Magazine in 2013 and "Best New Restaurant" in Rhode Island by the Providence Phoenix. Despite having an accomplished career, the biggest reward Nick has ever known has been the love of his family. It is for them that he stays driven to succeed. Thanks to the support and inspiration they provide he looks forward to expanding his portfolio as both a restaurateur and writer.

Made in the USA
Charleston, SC
07 November 2013